Gates of Hell Crossfire

Books by Stephen L. Thompson

The Crossfire Series

The SFO Series

Gates of Hell Crossfire

"Other than living really badly and dying poorly, just how does one get to Hell?"

Stephen L. Thompson

Gates of Hell Crossfire

The Crossfire team has been trained by God to stand against the enemy of mankind and their human tools over the last three years. Now they must stand against their own people as the Anti-Christ tightens his grip on the world and forces the American military to hunt the Team.

- Stephen L. Thompson

Gates of Hell Crossfire

Published by
Stephen L. Thompson
Facebook.com/CrossfireNovelSeries

Unless otherwise noted, Scripture quotations are taken from the HOLY BIBLE, NEW INTERNATIONAL VERSION®. Copyright© 1973, 1978, 1984 by International Bible Society. Used by permission of Zondervan Publishing House. All rights reserved.

ISBN- 978-1-943879-22-9

Published in the United States of America

Foreword

To my Christian readers –

The Crossfire series of action/adventure stories include depictions of violence which are unusual in Christian literature. It would be nice if there were no conflict or violence in our world. But we live in a time when evil is increasing instead of diminishing, when some men seem to be controlled by selfishness, madness, or evil forces. When the enemies of decent mankind are bent on subjugation of other men and women, righteous men and women must stand against evil. Please remember that the yoke of oppression is not lifted by prayer alone. God is our shepherd and we are his sheep. As long as there are wolves about, God will use some of us as sheep dogs to defend the rest of us. These stories are about people like that and the forces they fight against. The stories describe violence because it occurs in the real world and it is active in the lives of all people whether they recognize it or not.

To my non-Christian readers –

The Crossfire series include depictions of spiritual warfare and spiritual activity with which the non-Christian may not be familiar. These stories describe the realms and activities of both God and Satan because they are real and active in the lives of all people whether they recognize it or not.

Steve Thompson

CHAPTER ONE

Eli Moreh sat on a bench overlooking the quiet, peaceful Mediterranean Sea with Tel Aviv at his back. There was a soft, cool breeze blowing off the sea and the night sky was lit up by the lights of the city. As it had always been, it was a comfortable place. But, this time he came to this beach at what he was sure to be the end of his life. Although he was only twenty-eight years old he had run all he could, hidden as much as possible and finally, when there was no help for him and no one that cared about him anymore; he returned to a place where he had always been comforted and had wonderful times as a young boy.

Eli looked at the popular paved bike path behind him and to the South beyond his vision. The Tayelet in Tel Aviv is one of the main Tel Aviv attractions; a place to walk or run any time of night and day. It allows one to walk from the Tel Aviv Port all the way to Jaffa. This had always been a lovely place to sit and to enter the sea and swim. Nearby, there are many cafes and restaurants. His family had always stayed at the City Hotel in Tel Aviv when they came to this beach on vacation.

He realized that none of that really mattered this time. His parents were killed in an automobile accident and he had stepped in it big time and there was no longer any hope for him. During what he knew were the last few minutes of his life he came to a clear understanding of his mistakes. He had always thought that he could conquer any mountain and outrun any other person to the goal he was after. Not this time. Of course he was pretty sure that what was chasing him wasn't human.

His adult life had been exciting, always skating on the legal edge of the law and propriety. His computer forays into the most highly guarded places of Commerce and Government had shown him a different world than that of the news or the general public knowledge. He realized now that it was an insidious attraction to him and it had led him constantly onto bigger and more dangerous efforts.

His latest computer hacking had been his greatest accomplishment. It had promised him riches if he could sell the secret information to whoever wanted it the most. Oh yes, there had been warning signs he was getting too bold; but he had ignored them. After all, wasn't he, Eli Moreh, a power to be reckoned with? Well, now his ego was going to kill him.

This time he had entered in where he should not have gone and the powers that were protecting the information at this place were beyond anything he'd ever known and even though he managed to get the data, it was at too dear of a price.

This time Eli Moreh should not have thought too highly of himself. Now, he was also guilty of murder, not once, but three times! Even though he hadn't personally killed the three men; he had sought them out for protection and each one had died, horribly screaming while trying to stop the forces after him.

Now no one would help him anymore. The word was out that Eli Moreh was damaged goods and a target of unstoppable forces. He was a dead man walking and he could now sense that death approaching him as he sat on the bench looking out over the beach he had always enjoyed.

As the final tension was reaching an unbearable level, Eli heard voices. He looked to his right to the North and saw two young women walking along the Tayelet. The fear in him was very great but he could not let two completely innocent women die because of his mistakes. He knew what was coming for him would not care that two more innocent people died as it collected him. His eyes were dilated from the fear that filled his mind and he turned to look back toward the city in hopes there was nothing there other than his overwrought imagination.

What he saw scared him almost beyond his ability to move. The partial seen pursuers were horrible and terrifying, and now there were three of them. Evil radiated out of their eyes and drool dropped from their mouths as they grinned in anticipation of ripping him to pieces. Their misshaped bodies were large and dark and looked frightfully strong. Eli could see the claws and big knives they held as they moved out of the dark toward him.

Still, his personal code of honor would not be denied, even facing what he was. He looked at the women and yelled. "Get away!! Run for your lives! Do it now!" He was pointing to the North as the safest direction to separate them from the coming enemy and slaughter.

His heart sank as they continued to walk directly into the path of the monsters coming at him. He knew he would now be responsible for their deaths and worse. He would have to watch the horror as they died before his time came to die. He would have done anything to stop the slaughter about to happen.

What happened next was almost incomprehensible to him. He heard the two women start praying and with a blast of light both women were covered in bright golden armor from head to foot and they each had a sword of such brilliance that the entire beachfront lit up.

The terrors coming at him attacked the two women and were themselves chopped to pieces by the brilliant swords. They dissolved into a smoke and faded away. The armor and swords also faded from view and the beach was plunged back into night again.

Eli didn't know what happened or what he should do. He stood there as the two women prayed a short prayer and then walked over to him. He was able to stutter his thanks for their saving his life before his mind darkened, his knees gave out, and he sank to the ground. The two women walked around the bench and each one took one of his arms and easily lifted him from the ground and helped him onto the pathway to the North.

As they walked along, Eli's strength returned somewhat and he was able to walk unaided. His mind was still stunned by his salvation from sure death. He looked at the two women and realized they were very attractive and confident.

Eli finally understood that he wasn't going to die right then. He moistened his lips and asked no one in particular, "Who are you?"

The blonde woman gently said, "Relax Eli, we are here to help you. My name is Laura and this is Sarah."

Eli couldn't believe anyone would want to help him. "Who sent you?"

Sarah laughed. "Our boss, who you don't know, told us to bring you in out of the cold; stay close to us, there could be other attacks until we can get to a safe place."

The after effects of the whole event were beginning to set in on Eli and he felt weak again. "Can we please stop for a few minutes? I'm not sure I can keep walking right now."

Laura took his right arm again to support him. "Just a little farther and you can sit down."

They had already walked about eight hundred meters and as they walked around a grove of trees on the city side of the walk, Eli was stunned again. Sitting on the ground was an advanced Military helicopter with two soldiers standing outside of the craft with full combat outfits and holding large rifles.

The women led him up to the side of the helicopter, helped him into the body of the craft, and gently lowered him into a web seat. They buckled him into the seat. Sarah looked closely at Eli. "You're reacting to shock, this should help." She had a small aerosol bottle and she sprayed a mist into his face."

The soldiers got in and the blades started rotating. Very quickly the helicopter lifted off of the ground and rose into the sky. Eli had no idea where they were going and suddenly he didn't care anymore. A soft, warm darkness enveloped him and he relaxed hearing a lovely voice telling him that he was safe and he needed to rest.

CHAPTER TWO

Eli came to in a relaxed state where he could remember the fear but it seemed inconsequential to him. He opened his eyes and saw the woman called Sarah sitting across from him on a really nice couch. He shook his head in an effort to clear his thought processes and looked around. He thought, "I must be in a really high-priced hotel lobby. Everything is classy and beautiful with great lighting and I can see huge windows looking out on the sea."

He sat up and tried to straighten his clothes. Looking at Sarah he grinned. "I'm sorry I have been such a bother to you. But, to tell the truth I as lost as a goose. I don't know what has happened nor where I am, do you?"

Sarah looked at the young man with the messy hair. "You are in our base headquarters and you are safe. I'm going to have some other people come over and meet you. Perhaps we should speak English because most of these people don't speak Hebrew."

All Eli could think to say was, "Oh, okay, I guess."

Sarah kept watching him as she spoke into the air. "Eli is awake now if you would like to meet him."

Several minutes went by and three men came over and sat down by them. The youngest of the men smiled at him. "Hi Eli, my name is Ethan and I hear you had a pretty rough night."

Eli just nodded his head.

Ethan looked at the tallest man there and then back at Eli. "I guess I get to explain what is going on because we work in the same field, computers. Eli, you don't know me but we have worked together several times in the last two years."

Eli thought hard but couldn't place Ethan's face or voice.

Ethan continued, "I have followed your hacking career on-line with some interest and several times I accompanied you when you hacked into civilian and military data bases. Twice I facilitated your entry so that I could also investigate what was going on with that particular data base. One time I kicked you off so that you wouldn't be noticed and tracked. That was the time you tried to get into the U.S. National Clandestine Services group. They would have had you and your ID in several seconds and you would have had some unhappy visitors at your doorstep not too long after that."

Ethan shook his head, "I don't know what training or education you have, but you definitely have a knack for defeating data base defenses. I learned some things from you that have helped me. I thought I knew everything about the subject and I found I really didn't."

The tallest man there sat forward and reached out to shake Eli's hand. "Hello Eli, my name is Jack Malone and I head up this group. The reason we are involved with you is because you managed to weasel your way into an Iranian Military data base that we were interested in but hadn't been able to get past their firewall. That is also the reason that those killers were sent out to kill you. Our orders were to save you from them. I expect that those were not the only killers in the hunt for you and they don't like to quit until they achieve their goal."

Jack stared at him for a few seconds. "Let me ask you an important question. Were you able to get the files you went in to get?"

Eli thought about what had happened to him in the last three days. He definitely owed these people his life and maybe even more than that. He looked at Jack and nodded, "Yes, I got the files just before they burned the connection. I was going to sell the information, but I was able to understand a bit of the purpose of the project described in the file and I am not going to get rich at the expense of my country. It is beyond evil what they are planning and I dearly wish I had never hacked into that data base."

Ethan asked, "Do you still have that file?"

Eli nodded his head again. He reached down and undid his belt and slid an extremely small thumb drive out of a concealed pocket. He handed the drive to Ethan. Buckling his belt back together he sighed. "I have a sister who is a single mother with three kids. She is unemployed, and cannot get any public assistance. I was hoping to get enough from selling that file to get her a place to live and food for a while."

The third man sitting there was an older man that was a good dresser with style. He sat forward and offered his hand to Eli. "Eli, my name is David and I'm concerned as to why your sister can't get government help. Is it because she is a Messianic Jew?"

Eli looked angry and nodded. "Yes, and nobody wants to help her or the kids, not even God."

David looked at Jack and Ethan and nodded. He got up and walked away.

Jack took the thumb drive from Ethan and held it out in front of Eli. "If this drive contains the information I think it does, I can guarantee you that you and your sister will be well taken care of and be in a position to help other people like her."

Eli sat back and looked at the big man. "I don't understand. Aren't I in trouble for breaking into their database?"

Jack smiled, "Not with us. You may not realize it but God is helping your sister and arranged it so that you were the vehicle He used to do just that. Israel will be extremely grateful for this information and will reward you way beyond your wildest dreams. My team will see to it that they do."

Eli was a quick study and asked, "So, you're saying that God is using me to help defeat the evil that the Iranians are attempting to do to Israel and help my sister at the same time?"

Jack nodded his head. He spoke to Ethan as he handed the drive back to him. "I'll authorize a temporary entry pass for Eli, why don't you take him up to Charlie and dissect the data on this drive?"

Ethan jumped up and grinned. "Yes Sir." He motioned for Eli to accompany him and then stopped as Eli had trouble getting up. Ethan offered him a hand and got him to his feet. "Are you all right?"

Eli nodded, "I've just got to remember how to walk."

As the two young men walked off slowly toward the elevator, Jack asked, "What do you think, Charlie?"

Charlie's disembodied voice was clear. "Since there is no such thing as coincidence then I think I have a prospective employee. Let me see what we've got on that drive."

CHAPTER THREE

Eli was fairly overloaded with awe and surprises and took the multidirectional elevator with no comment. He went into a new level of unbelief when they exited onto the floor of the Communications and Security Group. The COMSEC floor would have awed the most advanced computer scientist. The air was cool and scented with a light mountain pine smell. It was very refreshing and elating.

To begin with, there was an extremely impressive line of CRAY Supercomputers against the back wall of the COMSEC Department. Ethan told Eli, "The Cray XC30 combines the new Aries Interconnect Intel® Xeon® processors, Cray's powerful and fully-integrated software environment. Innovative power and cooling technologies create a production supercomputer that is designed to scale high performance computing workloads of more than 100 pet flops. (1 quadrillion mathematical computations per second).

Then the workstations were amazing with their screens and control of massive operations all over the world. To Eli it looked like the people working at the workstations were in advanced lounger-style seats that were connected directly into the stations.

Suddenly Eli came face-to-face with a stern Asian man with his hand out. Eli stared at him for a second and then pointed over at Ethan. Ethan handed Charlie the drive and watched as he made a bee-line for his office. He looked at Eli, "Don't worry, that's Charlie Wu. He is the master of this domain and when he is on the hunt for a solution he forgets to be human." This was all said with a smile.

The two younger men walked over and watched through the glass of Charlie's office as he carefully reviewed the data on the drive and spoke to someone that wasn't there. Then he withdrew the drive and came out of his office. He handed the drive to Ethan. "Do your magic investigator guy thing." He looked at Eli and asked him if he would like to visit with him for a few minutes. Eli watched Ethan head to a workstation and then nodded and left for the office with Charlie.

Charlie asked Eli a series of work related questions and then thought for a few seconds. Making up his mind he turned to his computer keyboard and entered a series of commands.

Less than a minute later the three side-by-side 70-inch monitors above the desk line started to display a bewildering amount of information, photos, and graphics. Eli was stunned. All of this information was about him! The photos were from when he was a baby all the way up to a photo of him sitting in the chair in Charlie's office. He saw a list of every database he had hacked in the last five years and even when he had cracked his high school's computer to change his grades.

There was one screen that showed every medical thing that had ever happened to him and the results of operations, treatments, and dosages of every medicine he'd ever been prescribed. There was no part of his life that wasn't laid bare on the screens, including his romantic partners and their abbreviated histories and quirks.

Every vehicle and license he'd even just applied for was presented. His high school valedictorian speech was there in print and probably in sound too. It showed his income, or lack thereof for his whole life. He shook his head and looked at Charlie. "Who <u>are</u> you people? It would take me years just to find half of this stuff."

Charlie smiled and with one button wiped all the screens clear. "Eli, are you interested in a career? An exciting, well-paying, secure job?"

Eli was taken aback and grinned. "You want to offer a position to an ex-hacker who has a death warrant out for him?"

Charlie smiled again. "You're in good company. Every one of us here has multiple death threats against them. The critters that came to kill you last night want to kill all of us every day."

Eli shook his head, "How do you survive that?" His mind was whirling around with all the new things that were happening to him so fast.

Charlie sat back in his chair and studied the young man. "I'm a pretty good judge of character. Ethan was a much more active hacker than you when I hired him two years ago. He was one of my most productive computer personnel after that. And," Charlie waved his hand at the screens around him, "I have a pretty good history on everybody that works for us."

Eli chuckled, "And still you would hire a guy that broke into his high school computer to change his grades?"

Charlie grinned at the confused man. "I consider myself somewhat of a computer expert myself. I saw that you broke into that school computer to lower your grades, not to profit by raising them. Why did you do that?"

It caught Eli off guard that Charlie had picked up on that little twist. "Because my grades were so high I was going to be sent to a Special School for the Gifted and I didn't want to leave my family and friends."

Charlie grinned again. "Now that didn't work too well for you, did it? I saw that you were still valedictorian of your class."

It was Eli's turn to smile. "Oh, it worked just right. I was the top of my class, but, it was the still the class with all my friends and my parents were in the audience."

CHAPTER FOUR

Charlie made up his mind about Eli. "Okay, fun aside, do you want to hire on and make a difference in the world in a positive way?"

Eli realized his future was extremely short without these people around him so he said, "Okay."

Charlie nodded, "To be fair, I'm going to give you the information about our group and then I'm going to give you a second chance to answer that question."

"First, we are named the Crossfire Team and our charter is to obey God and defend mankind from Satan and his demons. The team is intimately connected to and anointed by God to do our job. We have the direct cooperation of the Israeli government and the Mossad. Our operations here in COMSEC are to define and support the missions our field teams have to handle. If you become one of the team by joining us, you will be in Satan's gun sights all of the time. Of course due to your actions with the Iranian's database, you are already in the enemy's gun sights."

"We have probably the most powerful computer operation in the world, at this point, and I expect we will continue to outgrow the other systems at an exponential rate for the next three years.

"While everyone in the Core Team and the Sensitive Operations Group or SOG are born-again Judeo-Christian or Messianic Jews and our allegiance is to the Father Yahveh, the God of Abraham, Isaac, and Jacob, and God's Son Yahshua, there is no requirement for the COMSEC personnel to follow our path unless they want to."

"Your formal training in computers and systems operations is sorely lacking, but you seem to make up for the classwork with a unique anointing of your own. We will provide training in the systems here and the unique capabilities that gives us input or control over everything from cell phones to satellites, ours or anybody else's. We have access to the latest and the greatest of equipment, software, and expertise."

"While you are in this base you are essentially safe from the demonic world because the base is protected twenty-four seven by angels from God.

"I see from your background you don't ascribe to any religion or system of faith. You don't have to do anything like that to work here, but I must warn you that the things you will see will probably give you the need to consider your relationship to God. Okay Eli, any questions?"

Eli blinked several times. Processing all the things that Charlie had given him had taken a few seconds. He looked at Charlie and asked, "Three things I need to know. First, what is the pay? Second, where are we? And lastly, what did you mean that we will continue to grow for the next three years. What happens after that?"

Charlie sat up in his chair. "I'm afraid I'll have to have your answer before I can respond to those questions. Otherwise we will have to use a neutralizer on you."

Eli hoped Charlie was joking about the ubiquitous "Neutralizer" from the Men in Black movies, where they brain-wiped everyone who shouldn't know what the MIB were doing. "Yes, I will join you and I will work my best and my hardest to achieve any goals you give me. I already owe this group my life once and I expect, based on your description of this operation, you are probably saving my life right now. Of course I will work for you." Eli was venting his irritation about how superior he thought these people were in relationship to him and his life.

Charlie had Eli fill out the appropriate paperwork which consisted of his signature only on preprinted forms with all of his information already filled out by the computer.

Charlie filed the data and turned back to his newest COMSEC employee. "Okay, first answer; your basic pay will be $100,000 U.S. dollars a year with bonuses. There are ways to increase that amount if you want to. Second answer; you are in a terraformed, geodesic bubble, one half mile under the Mediterranean Sea one half mile away from Tel Aviv. I'll explain all of the details later."

"Lastly, the reason I use the date of three years is because on a date roughly three and a half years from the time since the Rapture of the Faithful, the entire Crossfire Team is going to be called to Heaven to be with God. But, three and a half years after that we are expected to return with Yahshua and rule and reign with him for a thousand years."

CHAPTER FIVE

Eli nodded in acceptance of the things that Charlie told him. "What are my hours of work, where do I work, more importantly, where do I live?"

Charlie gave him a chart and outlined his hours of work, hours of training, and gave him a room number on the SOG floor for his domicile.

About that time Ethan came in with a large report and shook his head at Charlie. "You are going to go ape when you see what Major Abdullah has designed and our Damocles buddy Nazari is now in charge of. If the thing works, then all of Israel is in grave danger. We need a Core Team meeting at once."

Charlie called Jack and asked him to call the meeting. Jack said, "We will probably have to meet in about an hour. That will be right after Mark finishes his combat training for some of the new troops. Let's just make it one hour. I'll send out the message to the Core Team."

Charlie agreed and told Ethan to show Eli his room, work station, and whatever else he needed to start work on Monday after Shabbat.

Ethan took Eli in tow to accomplish Charlie's wishes. As they waited for the elevator Eli said, "I think I like Charlie, even if he seems a bit scary. Do you think he really likes me?"

Ethan laughed a hearty laugh. It took him a few more laughs before he could talk without interrupting himself. "My advice is to be grateful and to do whatever Charlie asks you to do. He can be your best friend or your worst nightmare. He demands your best and you need to give it to him. Also, I suggest you lose your cocky attitude about the people here in the team. You should realize how important their acceptance of you is to your future, let alone your future employment."

Eli said, "Okay, I will. But, he said that you were a bigger hacker than I was and I would have expected you to buck authority even more than I do."

They entered the elevator and the doors closed. Ethan then reached over and pushed the stop switch on the elevator.

Turning to Eli he made eye contact and spoke with real conviction. "Eli, you and I are not that far apart in age but I feel much older or at least much more mature than you."

"Charlie was a top security agent in China two or three years ago. That means that he was like a combination of an FBI agent and a CIA agent and an assassin who can kill you without getting up from his chair. I've seen him in combat and you really want the man on your side."

Ethan continued, "Yes, I was pretty deep into rebellion and anti-establishmentarianism and cocky like you until I got my original job with this group. I realized then that my attitude flew in the face of the people here. They were so humble, yet fiercely dedicated to their missions and the work they do. I would have looked like a spoiled little kid. So I acted properly while I watched and waited to see the façade come off and for them to act bossy and, shall I say, dumb as rocks."

Ethan sighed and smiled. "They never did and then I knew I wanted to be like them. Just two months ago I suggested we plant a sting and Trojan horse to throw off the people that they are fighting against right now. They liked the idea and gave me a chance to go out in the field with them to do just what I suggested."

"It was supposed to be an easy mission. Instead, I ended up fighting against other troops and demons, which I didn't think we're real up to the time I saw my first one. These people are for real and they demand that from everybody that works with them. Just to work here lets you do something that has eternal consequences for good. Don't let your disappointments in your youth and your attitude ruin it for you."

Ethan flipped the switch on the elevator and rode it in silence until they reached the SOG floor. Eli realized he had been saved by a really decent organization and mentally slapped himself in the head for thinking like an idiot. As the doors to the elevator opened, he stopped Ethan and shook his hand. "Thanks, I needed that right now."

Ethan smiled at him. "Just in case you are wondering if the people the Crossfire Team fights against are really the bad guys, OC or the Omicron Cartel are the people that blew up that mall in Georgia recently just to show how in control they are. They killed over three hundred totally innocent men, women, and children. They also rigged a second bomb that killed most of the first responders as they came to help the injured and wounded."

Ethan saw that Eli had gotten his message and he ended it with, "This is the team that took their International war machine apart and completely destroyed their leadership."

CHAPTER SIX

While Eli was being given the tour of the base by Ethan, Jack was addressing the Core Team in the War Room on the team's ongoing participation in the Kidon's Iranian challenge. "After praying for the Father's will in this matter we understand that He wants us to put a stop to the Iranian weapon that was created by Major Abdullah."

Jack put a picture of Nazari up on the large screen. "Bashan Nazari is a fairly inept Military Officer who just lost his boss, Major Abdullah, and the Sergeant who had been providing him with all of his Military ability at the same time. He doesn't know what to do or how to do it. The Iranian leaders decided that they didn't want Major Abdullah's project to be lost. After all, since receiving Nazari's glowing and clear reports on the project they had promoted the project so much that their fate is now tied to its success as much as is Nazari's.

After the misguided terrorist nuclear strike against their country there weren't too many talented leaders left who could continue the work and deliver the fatal blow to Israel. The wonderful reports from Bashan had clarified everything the Major had been doing. Therefore, since no one else had the full confidence and knowledge of the project with the exception of Bashan, the Military leaders promoted Bashan to the rank of Major and told him that it was his duty to complete the Major's project."

"Humbly accepting the new rank and duty Bashan was probably terrorized on the inside. He apparently has no clue as to how Major Abdullah was doing whatever he was doing on his project and now he doesn't have the Sergeant to tell him what to do. His promotion and assignment to lead the project to destroy Israel happened ten days ago. After the loss of the Major, it seems that Satan's demons have assumed control of all aspects of the project and have been told by Satan to tolerate Nazari as the apparent leader. This works well for the demonic because Nazari will die when he sets off the weapon in Israel in six days."

Mark sighed, "Does the Intel we acquired from Eli Moreh tell us what we are up against? What the weapon is supposed to do, and did Abdullah finish the development?"

Jack nodded, "It does describe the weapon and its effects. It does not tell us what the target is except that it is the Nation of Israel."

Mark asked, "Have we communicated the new information to the Mossad and what does the Kidon's Elon think of this new information? Does he trust it to be true?"

David answered Mark. "As soon as we deciphered the information on the disk we transmitted it to the Mossad. We haven't heard from them as yet."

Laura spoke up. "I somehow get the impression that all you guys know what the weapon is and what it does. Why don't I know about it?" This was presented as a question of curiosity, not irritation. Actually, Laura wasn't sure that she wanted to know.

CHAPTER SEVEN

Jack nodded his head. "What Major Abdullah created is a working death ray. It actually is an incredibly dangerous weapon against the Israelis. Based on Abdullah's short history as a creative terrorist, I would be willing to bet that he had no concept of the danger of this weapon. It is actually none of his design. The entire project is totally based on the work of several earlier Jihadist scientists that each tried to create a death ray before Abdullah ever thought of the idea. All of these earlier efforts failed miserably. In three of the four attempts the weapon killed the designer."

"Abdullah wasted three years and roughly twelve assistants trying different combinations of power sources, ray generators, and culminating lenses before he created a real working model. Understand that it is a working model in the laboratory, not in the field. Right now, it is the only working model."

"When I first read this data that Eli "borrowed" from the Iranian lab I was sure it was something that Nazari dreamed up or something he had read in a science-fiction magazine somewhere. But, after checking with Charlie and Doctor Clashire, I'm quite sure it is a real thing that can kill Israelis. You see, one of the vectors included in this "death ray" is a DNA-specific control. When the ray is pointed at a person and triggered; it only affects a person whose DNA matches the ray's vectors. Briefly, the ray gun will only kill people who have a specific genome that is unique to Israel."

Jack looked at the people around the table. "I'm saddened by the fact that Abdullah killed over thirty people with that specific DNA to prove the ray's selectivity and effectiveness. Three of those people were Kidon agents."

Mark asked, "Why don't the Iranians just make a big death ray generator with the specific DNA requirement and explode it over every city in Israel?"

Jack shook his head. "There is an inverse square of the distance limiting factor for the ray. It is not effective if it goes over thirty feet from the generator. Also, due to its enormous power requirements, it only allows for a single shot and then it takes thirty seconds to recharge the stored power cell for the next shot. So, it will be Nazari's role to prove the weapon in Israel on a one-at-time basis. His chances of succeeding and surviving are below one-half of one percent per Charlie's computer alter ego Crayton."

David snorted softly. "He probably won't get into the country anyway. But I sense that you're obliquely alluding to something more monstrous than one inept man trying to kill off the population of Israel one person at a time, right?"

Jack nodded his head and spoke into the air."Charlie, would you explain what you and Dr. Clashire concluded that makes this effort potentially much worse?"

Charlie's voice captured everyone's attention. "One of the dangers of terrorists' cobble-jockeying a solution based on many other people's dangerous works is that they don't have the scientific training to think through all the possibilities, so they usually can't see the forest for the trees."

"The scientific explanation for what I'm about to tell you takes eighty-five pages to summarize, so I'm going to give you guys the Cliff Notes version with a little background first."

"The word "radiation" refers to energy that emanates, or radiates from a source and travels through space with the possibility of depositing a fraction of its energy in any matter it encounters."

"There are many kinds of radiation. Familiar ones are radio waves that allow us to communicate long distances via phones, televisions, and satellites. Microwaves are used in communications as well as in microwave ovens. Visible light waves are those we can see reflected by matter, including raindrops that reflect the colors of a rainbow."

"These and similar types of radiation belong to the category known as non-ionizing radiation. They are considered non-ionizing because the individual waves have too little energy to cause ionization which is the stripping of electrons from atoms, which, in turn, breaks the chemical bonds of molecules, which give matter structure."

"Ionizing radiation, which is what we're talking about here, on the other hand, is capable of stripping electrons from atoms and breaking chemical bonds, creating highly reactive ions. These are atoms or molecules that have an electric charge. Radioactive materials, those that contain atoms that have unstable nuclei, occur naturally and emit ionizing radiation in a process known as radioactive decay."

"But, the most common types of ionizing radiation are alpha particles, beta particles, gamma rays, and x-rays. These particles and rays cannot be seen, heard, tasted, smelled, or felt, which is why ionizing radiation remained undiscovered until the late 1800s, even though many ordinary materials emit small amounts."

"Natural sources include the soil, water, air, food, and building materials. Man-made devices such as X-Ray machines also produce ionizing radiation. Potential sources include nuclear accidents involving medical or industrial nuclear material or terrorist or military actions involving nuclear devices."

"At high enough doses, ionizing radiation can damage molecules such as DNA in cells. Damage to DNA and other important cellular components can result in cell damage or cell death. This can lead to health effects like an increase in cancer risk and, at extremely high doses, death."

"This is where we see a high risk to everyone in Israel from this weapon. Remember I told you, *"Man-made devices such as X-Ray machines also produce ionizing radiation. Potential sources include nuclear...terrorist or Military actions?"*

"Recall that Jack and Mark detonated the two one-megaton warheads on the rocket-torpedoes that mystery submarine tried to launch less than three miles off of the beach at Tel Aviv? Well, it was hard to detect, but Crayton managed to determine that the atmosphere over most of Israel and the surrounding areas is covered in a massive amount of radiation-generated ionizing particles. These don't cause sicknesses such as radiation burns because that takes physical particles and those were mostly absorbed by the water and what got into the atmosphere blew away from Israel by the prevailing off-shore winds that day."

"But the atmosphere remains highly charged with ionizing radiation sources. Dr. Clashire feels that once Nazari activates this death ray machine it will detonate the surrounding atmosphere which will continue to detonate the atmosphere around it, and on and on. The ionizing particles will reproduce the activating waves until there are no more particles to detonate."

Charlie sighed this time and everyone heard the sadness in that sigh. "In other words, once Nazari pulls the trigger he will be killing everyone in the area of the highly charged ionizing particles which presently covers all of Israel, much of Egypt, Syria, and parts of Jordan, not to mention the camps at Palestine and the refugees in the area."

Mark asked Charlie, "I thought it only killed Jewish people with the right DNA."

Charlie was quiet for a few seconds. The he let the cat out of the bag. "Unfortunately for the rest of us, the DNA vector will probably not be replicated after the first firing of the "death ray".

"Between Dr. Clashire and Crayton, we've determined that that part of Major Abdullah's project was based on the NIL's work on a bomb that would only kill the children of people other than themselves. Actually, it was Satan's design and it would have killed all children in honor of Molec, the despicable god of fire. I thought the NIL and their factory disappeared completely in the fifty Megaton Hydrogen Bomb that obliterated their Jordanian base. Anyway, adding in that reaction to this one will result in one of two things. First, it will probably kill all human life in the area I just spoke of, or, it will flash ionizing radiation worldwide and kill all human life, even those that are underground."

CHAPTER EIGHT

Ethan Reaper thought about the consequences of Charlie's last statement. "Well, I guess that would be a major Rapture of a different kind."

Laura smiled, "I don't think you have to worry about either of the doomsday occurrences happening, Ethan. God's Word in the Bible has been exactly right on all the prophesies for the last six thousand years and Iran and Bashan Nazari aren't going to change the remaining prophesies or introduce any new ones. But, he could still kill a lot of God's people and we have to accomplish God's will to stop him from his warped destiny. Also, remember, Nazari doesn't want to do it, anyway."

Jack looked at Mark. "The Mossad and the Kidon don't believe in the New Testament prophesies so I think we need to make contact and see what we can do to help them snag Nazari before he hurts himself or others."

Mark nodded and pointed at David and Sarah. "Let's go visit Director Tzahal again."

Mark called ahead and got permission to meet with the Mossad Director. They arrived in time to catch an elevator as they walked into the building.

Mark, David, and Sarah were ushered into the Director's office and greeted him. He indicated that they sit down and wait a few minutes. Elon of the Kidon came into the office and sat down, also.

Mark kicked the meeting off. "Director, Elon, I'm glad that we have time to meet today. Did you get the information we sent you?"

The Director nodded. "Yes we got the information. But, I do wish that you had called us and allowed the Kidon to accompany you when you collected Mr. Moreh. Were you expecting to "get a jump" on us by acting alone?"

Mark was somewhat taken aback by the implied hostility by the Director. "I'm sorry that we didn't invite you but, no, we didn't expect to get a "jump" on you at all."

Elon spoke up. "I've read your files extensively, Mr. Connelly, and your track record indicates that you prefer to prosecute your cases by yourself before you tell anybody else what's going on."

David sensed the animosity between the Kidon and the Crossfire Team and attempted to defuse the feelings of all parties. "Director, Elon, Mark, I thought that we were going to work as a team instead as competitors."

Elon was obviously upset and couldn't back off of his critical nature about this one-upsmanship by the team. "I thought so too, until Mark Connelly's true colors came out when he had to get to the lead by himself before anyone else heard about it!"

Mark started praying to find out what this was all about. He quickly got a solid leading and relaxed. He stood up and was matched by David and Sarah. He smiled at Elon and spoke to the Director. "I understand your stress concerning everything you or we do about this Iranian plot. Just to help you cool your jets, I will tell you that the Kidon could not have saved Eli Moreh's life if they had been there because there were demons involved and that is our part of the deal."

"Also you need to check your facts before accusing me of trying to take your first look capability away so that I get credit for it. I wasn't involved at all. Sarah and Laura took out the demons and got Eli to our base where Charlie and Ethan handled him. I haven't even met the man, yet. Although I did hear that Charlie hired him. Also, there is a good chance that Major Abdullah's death ray could kill all Israelis if he gets one shot at anybody. From now on we will let you get the first look on your own and still back you up if you need us. Have a good night."Mark turned and walked out of Director Tzahal's office with David and Sarah right behind him.

As they reached the elevators, Elon ran up to them. In anger he shouted at Mark, "Look, I don't like your attitude and..." He lost his voice when he found himself being slammed to the floor by Sarah. As he started to react to that act he found David's pistol next to his temple. David's voice was soft but icy cold. "You need to rethink your attitude Elon. As one of the Mossad's killer elite you should recognize that Mark's wife is unhappy with you and your lifespan at the present moment is measured in milliseconds."David stood up and made his handgun disappear.

Elon looked into Sarah's eyes and found no compassion there. She was still standing quietly between him and Mark, but Elon saw the glint of the throwing knife in her right hand. He lay back down on the floor and stayed quiet.

Mark and David entered the elevator and Sarah said one sentence to Elon and then joined them. The doors closed and Elon found the Director Tzahal standing above him. The Director was still looking at the closed doors of the elevator and asked Elon. "What did she say?"

Elon rose to his feet and brushed himself off. "She said, "Don't ever come at Mark in anger again. This <u>was</u> your last chance."

The Director nodded his head. "That was very good advice Elon. You would be wise to heed it."

Having realized his mistake due to his uncontrolled anger, he agreed silently and nodded.

CHAPTER NINE

As the elevator descended from the Director's floor David looked at his hands and said, "I wonder if Elon realizes just how close he came to dying tonight?"

Sarah looked at her friend and he read the tightly controlled rage in her eyes. "It was actually an extra chance because he had already wasted his last chance. I only resisted killing him because Director Tzahal was coming up behind him. I'm glad he saw that conviction in my eyes and didn't challenge me."

Mark decided he needed to cool his wife's anger before it spilled over onto the next person they met. He knew how tightly she was wound up so he slowly and carefully put his hand around her shoulders and pulled her over to him. He said softly, "I am very proud of you and the fact that you always have my back. God loves you so much and He has given you great and terrible talents to dispense death or give life. I'm glad you spared Elon, and the fact that you probably scared the anger out of him for a long time. Did I tell you that I am SO glad you're on my side?"

Sarah melted into Mark's embrace and let the passion dissipate as she prayed for forgiveness from the Savior for her anger. She confessed it as sin, and repented of it. She didn't tell Mark that she had checked with God and she had already had His permission to take the Kidon killer out if necessary. She would keep her peace about this subject and let God work out the details. But, she would keep her eyes on Elon.

After the three team members described the confrontation to Jack and the rest of the Core Team they redesigned their efforts to one of assistance when asked for from the Kidon or the Mossad. Jack then set the rules for their own operation. "We will continue to monitor the situation and if the Kidon is too high and mighty to ask for help, we will have to act on our own. We have been charged by the Father to stop Nazari and the demons involved in this action from activating Major Abdullah's death ray in Israel."

"We stop reporting our efforts until they require our assistance. But, we will act unilaterally if needed. These people are our charges if not our buddies. Just because they don't understand Satan's plans for God's people, we do. Instead of getting into a territorial dispute, we will pray and follow the Father's will regardless of the ignorance of our hard-headed friends."

After the entire Core Team prayed, they felt led to continue the battle but no one received directions or a leading as to how to continue.

Laura was still praying when she got a word from the Lord. "Guys! The Father is moving us into a new level of operation. We need to use our past experience, our tools, and our weapons to resolve God's will in this matter rather than asking for directions."

Jack smiled at that. "She's right on this." He keyed his microphone and asked for Carol Moffet. Carol responded and said that she would be right there.

After arriving and taking her seat, Carol looked at Laura, "Laura, you have truly heard from the Father and the demonic is not happy about that, actually they are highly upset about it. The Father in Heaven has tasked me to provide the team with direction on how to combat Nazari and Major Abdullah's weapon based on my study of the spiritual Matrix of actions"

Carol thought for a few seconds. "First, Nazari is changing his time table since the demons have convinced him that Israel is aware of his original schedule. He will accelerate the time for the activation of the weapon to avoid our use of his plans. Second, Satan is going to do a "full-court press", as the basketball types or coaches would say."

"The Matrix shows that Nazari is going to have a legion of demons surrounding him and protecting him from detection so that he can succeed in his plans to use Abdullah's "death ray". Thanks to Charlie Wu's development of his demon tracker software we should be able to determine his exact location. Be aware that there will be numerous decoy formations of demons, because they know about our technology and will attempt to mislead us."

"Lastly, the Father gave me a message for the team. *"My children are in grave danger. I will not allow this to happen and I am depending on your team to stop the Iranians from using this most evil weapon on my chosen people. Do not be concerned with the attitudes of the Kidon about demons. I shall be glorified by this action and all will see that I am God."*

CHAPTER TEN

Bashan Nazari had explained how the Israel Death Ray worked to four different levels of Iranian Military management. He only had four days left on Abdullah's original schedule before he had to be in Israel to pull the trigger on the device. He had done everything he could to get out of being the test goat but no one else wanted to have the opportunity either.

He had resigned himself to doing his duty even if he couldn't understand why _he_ had to do it. But, he would be ready and walk off the ship at Jaffa and find the person he had to kill.

Even his wealthy Saudi father couldn't help him or buy his way out of this "honor" as a Hero of Iran. He sighed for the umpteenthtime today. He had started his religious rites again and prayed the five daily prayers to God and had asked for release from this deadly game he had to play. He had no answer and time marched on without hope.

Two days later there had been an equally frustrating time in Israel as the Kidon reported to their Director. Abram Cahn could tell that Elon was discouraged, mad, sad, and feeling ineffectual for the first time in his career with the Kidon. Elon shook his head and talked about the cause of all these emotions. "There is no way that anything works! We have tried to locate Nazari. We desperately want to stop or kill him. But, we are being beaten at every turn. Our in-place agents are running scared and have taken to hiding from us. Our own operatives die or are completely rebuffed at anything they attempt! We have killed three Iranian Military Aides with sticky bombs trying to kill Nazari. We knew which vehicles he always uses. We planted the bombs and he took different vehicles this one time. It is like they know everything we are doing before we do it!"

Director Cahn was angry and showed a distinct unhappiness at the report. "The man is coming here in two days! It is totally unacceptable that we can't stop him. I have to talk to my superior and tell him that there is nothing we can do. We have had this case for the last three weeks and we're farther from a solution than we were then. Do nothing more until I return."

That afternoon the Kidon Director Cahn met with his Mossad boss Hiram Tzahal and described the situation to him. The Director of the Mossad listened carefully to the entire report and asked for clarification on several points. He pondered the consequences for a few minutes and then made up his mind. He opened a drawer in his desk and took out a letter. He handed it to the Kidon Director and told him to read it.

After reading the letter twice, the Kidon leader threw the letter onto the desk and asked, "How? How can they have known?

The Director of the Mossad smiled a faint smile. "Because that is what they do. They have seen this exact situation dozens of times in the last four years. You need to seek their help. Do it quickly because our scientists agree with theirs and there is a chance the device will cause wide-spread death among everyone in Israel if it isn't stopped before it is used."

The Kidon director nodded his head and got up to go back to his department. On the way there he made a phone call to an old friend.

Three hours later Elon sat in a chair and asked forgiveness for his attitude and actions the last time they had met.

David Zahavy accepted Elon's apology for the Crossfire Team and asked what the Mossad and Kidon were doing to prevent Bashan Nazari for getting into Israel.

Elon cited all the normal precautions and the elevation of watchfulness at all shipping ports, airports and borders. "But", he added, "We both know that if someone wants to get into our country there are always ways to do it undetected. Sympathizers and in-place agents of the enemy are constantly working to bring in bombers and terrorists. If Nazari comes here he will probably have help finding a way to bypass our efforts to stop him."

David nodded, "Especially if he has spiritual covering from the demons that are running this show. They were able to smuggle a multi-megaton nuclear warhead into the Houston, Texas area of America and detonate it with ease and we both know that the Americans have an excellent defense against the introduction of nuclear weapons into their country."

Elon suppressed his normally caustic remarks about people that believe in mythical demons and their effects. "Then how do we fight against this?"

David knew Elon's background and training that went against believing in anything that the majority of Rabbis denounce, which included demons in our dimension. "Let us first go and talk with Rabbi Chanan. Then let's go to the Sea Base and talk to Charlie. He has created a way to detect demonic activity and to track it. We know from the Father that the Iranians have already accelerated the schedule, so that means Nazari is most likely already in Israel and is preparing to strike his target. After all, the demons that are stopping your activities have surely told the Iranians that we have the original timetable."

CHAPTER ELEVEN

Unable to see the Rabbi due to scheduling conflicts, David sent a text to Charlie that he and Elon were coming to discuss the plans to find and stop Bashan Nazari. He also included Mark, Sarah, Jack, and Laura as blind copies on the text.

They arrived at the Portal and processed through and down to the base itself. As they crossed the airfield and entered the Crossfire Team part of the base they met Jack and Mark coming out of the entrance tunnel. David was especially on guard to prevent any recriminations or bad feelings between Elon and Mark.

Elon shook hands with both of the team leaders and asked Mark to forgive him for his unacceptable actions and comments of the last meeting. Mark smiled at the man. "Certainly, I forgive you. No hard feelings?"

Elon agreed and admitted that his reactions had delayed the cooperative efforts to stop Nazari. They started to go their own ways when Mark said, "Elon, wait a minute. I want you to have this."

Elon turned back to Mark expecting and ready for anything. Mark reached into one of his pants pockets and pulled out a NovaStar II medallion and handed it to him. Then he hurried out to catch up with Jack.

Elon looked at the medallion with a question on his face. David smiled, "That is an identifier for the NovaStar defense system in our part of the Sea Base. It lets the lethal system know that you are a friend and not an enemy. It will allow you to fight with it and avoid destroying you if it is employed."

Elon nodded his head realizing the trust implied by Mark by giving him the medallion. He hung the medallion around his neck. It dawned on him that he really needed to change his attitude about these people, especially Mark.

As they walked along the inlet tunnel Sarah came out of a side alcove and walked by them and said "Hi."

David and Elon returned the greeting and kept going. David was sure that Elon didn't miss the message from

Sarah. She was carrying an IsraeliDSR1 Bull Pup sniper rifle and she was unloading it as she walked. Elon muttered, "A good woman to know."David quietly responded, "A good woman not to tick off."

Elon nodded his head in agreement as they stepped into the elevator to go to the Communications and Security floor on floor 5.Walking into the COMSEC department, Elon was very impressed with the high tech represented throughout the department. He didn't understand how they could get windows that looked out on the sea that was almost a mile above them. He thought he'd inquire about that later.

Charlie met them at his door and invited them to grab some chairs and they'd go over the Crossfire Team's investigation into Nazari's location at present. Charlie brought up the current satellite view of the Nation of Israel. There was a lot of data represented but Charlie wiped that off the screen to focus on their objective.

Elon was a specialist in data compilation and display and he had a photographic memory. Some of the data on that initial screen was considered "eyes-only top secret to Israel", including things like nuclear weapons and stockpiles that Israel insisted did not exist. Also shown had been most of the secret border protection emplacements.

Elon realized that the Crossfire Team had probably been in possession of that information for more than three years and the Mossad had never known that the Crossfire Team possessed it. Elon also knew that they hadn't misused their knowledge, either. There was no known use of this information like leaks or releases to the press. His estimation of the team's abilities and their protection of Israel's secrets went up another notch. Added to that it was impressive to Elon that Charlie was using a top secret Israeli satellite in this demonstration.

Charlie brought up an overlay that highlighted five or six positions showing a dozen or so whirling graphics in various places around Israel. He asked Charlie what they represented.

Charlie smiled, "Those, my friend, are representations of demons active in our dimension. Our problem is discovering the true group of demons guarding and supporting Bashan Nazari and eliminate wasting our time responding to the decoys."

David spoke to Elon with passion. "When we determine the right group we need to time it out so that our group and your flying squads go into battle at the same time. One of those demons can easily kill all of your team's personnel and they would do it without a qualm. I've seen these vermin kill highly trained soldiers in Italy, Germany, England, the United States and here in Israel. They are real and right now we are one of only twelve groups in the world we know of that has been anointed by God to battle demons on equal terms. Do you understand? Timing this out correctly is not a ploy to allow us to be first or an attempt to steal the publicity of the investigation."

David continued, "We, like you, work in the background and never seek publicity. I have fought these things many times and they have the ability to come out of their dimension and attack suddenly without warning. The ones that have God's approval to come into the human dimension are bullet proof, bomb proof, and cannot be stopped by normal Military means. They are stronger and more evil than a person can rationally understand."

Elon was becoming less sure of his position about demons all the time he was here. No one that had the resources, capabilities, and personnel that this team had would try to make people believe in phony demons. This was what Elon originally thought they were doing. They believed that these demons were real and yet they were humble about their role in defeating them. Elon could feel a major change in his worldview coming at him very fast.

Charlie commented, "Demons are evil and powerful but not very smart. We can discount the groups away from Tel Aviv and Jerusalem as decoys. There is not enough concentration of targets in those areas. There are three groups in the vicinity of Tel Aviv and two groups near Jerusalem. Now, how can we discern which one is the correct group hiding Nazari?"

Elon had determined to consider the whirling patterns as enemies and try to determine which one was the group with Nazari. He thought about the placement of the three groups around Tel Aviv and noticed a pattern that would have given away a human effort to muddy the waters. "The upper left group and the group to the far East of downtown keep moving around. The one to the South of the city is holding fixed and has, since you brought them up on the screen.

David nodded, "Elon is right. That would probably be the real group. I notice the ones in Jerusalem are also continually moving, too. Good catch Elon."

Charlie called Mark. "Mark, I think we have identified the group of demons with Nazari. They are South of the Portal and hovering around Balfour Street and Sderoi Rothschild Highway. I'll send you a map."

Elon suddenly made the connection. "They are there because Hiram Stein is there! He is speaking at the Azriel Center today with the American Ambassador to Israel on a new defense pack that targets Iran as a terrorist nation."

Charlie passed that information onto Mark and asked Elon, "Are they in talks now? And, if so, when will they be done?"

Elon looked at his watch. "They are talking right now and they will talk to the press outside the building on the Rothschild side in about one hour. Don't you see? They can't get through the security in the building but the public is allowed to approach the dignitaries at the press conference that is held after the meeting. That's got to be where Nazari will unleash his weapon to destroy Hiram Stein!"

David told Elon, "Set up your flying squads and meet the Crossfire Team there at 1:45 sharp. Meet one block south of the intersection the demons are on. Be very stern in warning the flying squads not to attempt to attack until we are there. That is, unless you want to bury them all in closed caskets."

Elon dialed the emergency number and talked rapidly in Hebrew for several minutes. David listened to ensure the Kidon warriors would coordinate with the Crossfire Team prior to assaulting Nazari. By then they could hear the alarm spreading throughout the Crossfire part of the Sea Base. The Core Team and the SOG were rushing for their aircraft in full battle gear. Charlie was putting on his armor and helmet.

Elon had seen the activity inside the base on Charlie's screens and asked David as they ran out of the COMSEC area, "Why is your team taking so many people?"

David was running for the Armory to get his battle gear and Elon was staying with him. David told him, "We were warned that there is a legion of demons defending Nazari. In Christ's time a Roman legion had between four thousand to sixteen thousand troops. There is going to be a major battle in a few minutes. Just hope we can win this one or Nazari is going to accomplish his task and possibly kill every Jewish person that we live to protect as well as those we love."

CHAPTER TWELVE

As David and Elon ran for the aircraft, one of the Mossad personnel from the other side of the Sea Base ran out to meet them and gave Elon his body armor and weapons. After looking at the people of the Crossfire Team the man also took also took off his helmet and gave it to Elon.

The giant rotors on the three MV-22 Osprey tilt rotors were whipping the air as the first two lifted off the runway and headed for the exit tunnel. David and Elon ran up the rear loading ramp and into the jammed interior as the ramp was raised and their Osprey lifted off the runway and followed the other two aircraft.

Elon checked his weapons and saw a seasoned IDF soldier he knew, crouched near the ramp. Elon squatted down next to the man and shook hands with him. In Hebrew he asked the man if this was his first time fighting with the Crossfire Team. The man shook his head, "No Sir, I fought with them at the Portal invasion six months ago. I have seen no more dedicated and fierce warriors than these people. Especially if there are demons involved. I also helped stop the mini-invasions at the border three months ago. If there hadn't been one of them there with their armor and sword to fight the demons, I wouldn't be here."

Elon again shook the man's hand and got up. Looking around he found David and leaned against the wall with him as the seats were all taken. "Apparently, your team gets high marks from the IDF warriors that have fought with you before."

David was a veteran of many battles for Israel, personally and spiritually. "You'll soon see that the team lives up to its reputation. I'm personally amazed at the Mossad and IDF forces we fight with frequently."

Elon asked, "Why, do you feel that way after having served in the Mossad and fought with these same forces for years?"

David looked at Elon. "Even after seeing these demons that their rifles and handguns can't affect, they stand their ground and battle on without the armor and swords that God has given our team. It is comparable to taking on a tank that you know you can't hurt with your weapons but you make yourself stay out there. Because you will do anything you can to slow it down even knowing it can take your life easily at any time. That is true heroism in defense of Israel."

The three Ospreys sat down in the street in a staggered row with their ramps open and locked down by touchdown. The troops moved out and along with the flying squads of Mossad and Kidon troops and they were placed into position by Mark Connelly.

Checking his time, Mark signaled "Advance" and led the troops North toward Balfour Street at double time. Elon noticed that the Israeli citizens had seen the signs and had done a very efficient self-evacuation of the area. He realized it didn't take them long to understand the Military aircraft and the armed troops meant trouble and they quickly decided to be somewhere other than here.

As they ran David touched his arm and Elon looked at him. "Shoot head shots on every demon you see."

Elon asked "Why?"

David shrugged his shoulders. "I don't think God would give Satan the right to send a legion of demons into Tel Aviv so most of the demons we see will probably be here illegally and that makes them vulnerable to bullets and bombs. Let the Crossfire Team handle the ones that are invulnerable to your bullets or grenades."

The troops slowed to a halt and squatted down. Elon and David made their way to the front of the group. Mark waved them over to his position next to Charlie. Charlie showed them the satellite view of the area. Elon could still see the whirling patterns but he could also see a red dot in the middle of the other patterns. Charlie pointed to the dot. "That's Nazari and he will be here in about eight seconds."

Right on time a single man with a trench coat came walking down Balfour Street on the sidewalk away from the waiting troops. He was obviously hiding something under his coat and was so focused on his objective he did not notice the men crouched down across the street in the shadow of a building. He also hadn't noticed the lack of people around him. Mark told Elon, "You take him down; we'll work on the demons."

Elon got up and walked across the street to intercept the terrorist. He noticed that Mark and Sarah were keeping pace with him, but one step back. They had given him the job to stop the "death ray" but were backing him up in case.

As he neared Nazari the man noticed him. Nazari realized that his real nature was known and he tried to pull a large device out from under his coat, but it was hung up on the cloth. Elon was about to shoot him when a demon manifested between him and Nazari. Elon suddenly decided that demons were real.

The evil radiating from the beast was almost matched by the horrible odor wafting away from its degenerate body. The beast was gross, ugly, and repulsive on all levels and it was armed with a large black sword. Elon could see the murderous desire to kill him in the three eyes of the beast. The fact that it was at least eight feet tall and five feet wide added to the fear factor. But, Elon had been on many battlefields and wasn't going to scream in fear and run despite the fact that he knew beyond the shadow of a doubt that he was about to die. As instructed, he shot the creature in the head and watched as nothing happened. The horrible creature ignored the shots completely and raised its sword to cut Elon in two.

Out of his peripheral vision he saw Sarah, now covered in golden armor from her head to her feet. She had a shield and a gleaming sword that sang a song of Heaven as the Esteem of Yahveh rolled off of the blade in waves. She stepped next to Elon and he could see the Wrath of God in her face and eyes. She raised her sword and the mighty black blade shattered into pieces when it struck the brilliant blade of God held by Sarah.

Mark had also stepped forward and ran the creature through the chest with his sword. He was covered in armor of a brilliant silver color that matched Sarah's golden armor and with Mark's additional muscle mass it was even more imposing. The demon dissolved into a red smoke and disappeared completely.

Elon was so stunned he just stood there. Mark raised one silver encased arm, pointed at Nazari, and said, "Please shoot that Oysvurf!" (Yiddish for a bad person). Nazari had also stopped moving and was standing there staring. It was probably the first time he had seen a demon. It had frightened him beyond his ability to function.

Elon raised his rifle and carefully shot Nazari in the forehead. The force of the round that killed Nazari also slapped his body to the ground. His nerveless fingers had dropped the "death ray" device and Elon shot it several times to make sure it was unusable to anyone.

The rest of the troops charged into the street and formed into two groups. The Crossfire Team moved into the foreground and each person started to pray. Thirty-eight sets of gold or silver armor appeared along with the shining swords as the warriors stood forth to do battle against Satan's demons that began to materialize.

The remainder of the Kidon and IDF troops formed a "U" shaped formation that surrounded the Crossfire Team. It seemed like the sky suddenly opened and poured out demons of all kinds. The volume of rifle and grenade fire was enormous as the Israel contingent did its best to shoot every demon they saw. The demons that didn't die came right at the warriors of the Crossfire Team.

Elon fired until he didn't have any more ammunition and then marveled at the Holy Anger filling the Crossfire warriors. They were killing demons by the dozens and then moving on to fight more demons. Sometimes they went so fast they were just a blur of motion and sword blades.

Twice Elon had to dodge demon blades and both times he registered that Sarah or Mark appeared and killed the demon before rushing back into the battle. But it became obvious to Elon that they were tiring after dispatching hundreds of demons and the demons were getting closer to overwhelming the warriors each second.

Elon looked around and found one of the IDF soldiers had been killed and was on the ground. Elon grabbed the man's rifle and found it full. He started shooting demons in the head as fast as he could. He picked up two more magazines and reloaded again and again. He was not going to let these valiant warriors die. He kept firing at demons until there were no more demons to shoot. He dropped the rifle and stood there exhausted but elated. There were only a few of the indestructible type in the battle any more.

He sensed more than saw a large demon appear next to him and Mark and Sarah were too far away to defend him. He didn't care at that point. He had done his duty to God and Israel and knew he would be all right regardless. He turned to face the horror about to kill him with a defiant smile.

As the black blade flew at him there was a burst of gold and fierce white. The black blade was struck down. The back hand swing of the shining blade struck the head off of the demon.

The sudden reversal of his situation left him completely stunned but happy. He looked to his right; sure he would see Sarah only to see a beautiful angel smiling at him.

Elon said, "Why did you save me?"

"The father said of you; *"Because he loves me," says the* Lord, *"I will rescue him; I will protect him, for he acknowledges My name."*

She whirled into a flurry of brilliant white mixed with pure gold and faded from view.

Elon started crying and slowly sank to his knees on the battlefield. It was tears from his heart that ran down his face as he gave grateful thanks to Yahveh for sending an angel to save him from death by a demon from Hell.

Many things had suddenly changed for him, today. His beliefs, his worldview, his pride and ego, and his choice of friends.

CHAPTER THIRTEEN

Sarah and Mark came over to where Elon was sitting on the ground weeping. Their armor had faded out after the last demon had been dispatched. They sat down on either side of him and each of them put an arm around his shoulders.

After a few minutes Elon stopped weeping and wiped his eyes and scrubbed his face. He patted each of them on their back to let them know he was all right. Mark said, "Welcome to a wider war, brother."

Sarah asked him if he was really all right. Elon nodded and continued to sit there as the troops collected their dead and wounded and the Tel Aviv police moved in to clean things up. Elon noticed that Mark had picked up the death ray gun and set it on the ground in front of them. Elon stared at it and asked, "Does this mean the end the war?"

Both Mark and Sarah said, "Oh no, of course not." Mark continued, "This was but a skirmish. This was one battle out of many. But I want to congratulate you on taking it all in stride. You stuck in there and helped us even the odds and eventually defeat the demons badly enough that they ran home with their tails between their legs."

Sarah laughed, "Yeah, the ones that had tails and/or legs."

Elon said, "I saw a beautiful gold and white angel. She saved me from that last demon and destroyed it."

Sarah said, "Yeah, that was Rose. She is one of our guardian angels. We see her a lot with messages from the Most High and in combat. Hang around us long enough and you'll probably get to meet Caleb, our other guardian angel. Better yet, you might get to meet Yahshua in person."

Elon sharply looked at Sarah, "You really mean that? You've met Yahshua? He really is alive? You met him in person?

Sarah looked seriously at Elon. "In our battle near the Kremlin, in Russia; Laura, Jack, and I were seriously wounded and Mark and several others of the team had been killed by demons. I was barely conscious when Yahshua appeared. He rebuked an Arch-Angel level demon and sent him to the pit until time for his judgment. He then told us that we had been faithful and true and the Father wanted us all healed. I passed out at that point. When we woke up, we were all healed and Mark and the others were healed and alive again."

Sarah shook her head, "Another time in Siberia, Russia, Laura had been mortally wounded by a demon blade and she was dying as she and Jack were falling on a piece of busted off balcony into a fire thirty-five feet below. A Russian General who was helping us had just been shot to death when a bullet went through my throat. I was bleeding out and in the process of dying when the Father saved and healed us again."

Mark added, "You definitely get to meet all sorts of interesting people in this job."

Elon nodded his head, "It also sounds like Russia isn't a great place to visit."

Mark got up and offered a hand to Sarah and the other hand to Elon. As he pulled them up he smiled. "Not our favorite place either, buddy. But, we go where the Father sends us."

Elon picked up the damaged death ray device and they walked back down the street they had come up before the battle and over to the last of the three Osprey aircraft. After they climbed on board the ramp was raised and the Osprey lifted up off of the street. The three tired warriors found an open space on the floor and settled down for the short ride.

Mark noticed that the pilot was maxing out the engines to get them back to the Sea Base and was about to go up and find out why when Megan Cole came back and knelt down in front of all three of them. "I'm supposed to tell you that your battle com isn't working, again, and that we are hauling our tail back to beat the advent in several minutes of two spy satellites which are coming over the horizon and could see us going in under the island."Mark nodded his acceptance of the reason for the hurry.

CHAPTER FOURTEEN

After the Osprey landed and the passengers disembarked Elon turned to Mark and said with great sincerity, "I apologize for anything I've said or done to criticize you or the work of your team. Please, believe me when I say that I didn't know..."

He stopped talking after Mark grinned at him and told him "Elon, I went through the same thing you are going through right now and it is embarrassing but cathartic to your soul. Whatever happened before today is not important to me or to my wife. You showed us your true character on the battlefield today. When you were faced with an enemy you couldn't kill you found weapons and stood tall anyway. That really did a lot to help us. I can tell you that God bonded you to our team today. The proof of that statement is that He allowed one of our guardian warrior angels to defend you against the enemy.

Elon nodded his gratitude. "If there is time in the next week or so I would gratefully sit down with you and discuss Yahveh and Yahshua."

Mark tipped his head and thought. "That's good; I'll make time, if I ever get enough rest to talk coherently."

Mark and Sarah shook hands with Elon and parted friends and fellow warriors who had shared combat.

Mark turned in his armor and realized it was completely covered with demon stain. He wondered how the rest of him looked. He sat down at a table in the Armory and dictated his after-action report because he knew he'd forget some of it by tomorrow morning.

He trudged up to his and Sarah's apartment and stripped down. He had a hot shower and cleaned up. Putting on casual clothing he walked out to the bedroom to find Sarah sitting there in her under-armor and completely asleep. Knowing Sarah's propensities and her capabilities, he spoke to her from across the room. "Hey, Spy Lady, you want in the shower now?

Sarah snapped awake with a knife in her left hand and a handgun in her right. Mark noticed that the gun was solidly pointed at him. Sarah relaxed as recognition overcame her training and she lowered the weapons and sort of grinned at her husband. "You are one smart man; waking me up from over there."

Mark walked over to her and hugged her as she rose to get cleaned up. He kissed her neck and she pulled away and looked at him. "What, my lips aren't good enough for you?"

Mark shrugged, "Actually, that spot I kissed on your neck is just about the only clean place on you right now." He looked at her and shook his head. "I've been married to you for over three years now and I still don't know where you hide that pistol. I mean, for God's sake woman, you're in your underwear and still have a hide-out gun and a knife! How do you do that?"

Sarah showed a mysterious grin and said, "A woman has to have some secrets, you know. She went into the bathroom still grinning and carrying both weapons.

After showering twice to get the sweat and demon stain off of her, she took care of her skin and pulled on a night shirt and went back to the bedroom.

Mark was still sitting up in bed waiting for her. She could tell the poor man was so tired he couldn't keep both eyes open at the same time. She slid under the covers and cuddled up against him as he finally lay down under the covers and she kissed him on the lips. He put his arms around her with a happy sigh and immediately went to sleep.

CHAPTER FIFTEEN

The next morning Mark felt revived and very hungry. He was alone in the apartment so he went down to the dining area. Sarah had found six women and one man already in the kitchen making a huge breakfast for all the newly awakening warriors.

Everyone was hungry and the food went down quickly. In less than thirty minutes the dishes were done and Sarah joined Mark at a table and they found themselves alone. Sarah smiled and kissed the back of Mark's hand. She said, "You know, I thought the reason you waited up for me as tired as you were was because you were going to frisk me to find out where I hid my gun."

Mark smiled back, "Dang it! That was what I was going to do. Somehow it got lost in the moment. Did you get enough sleep?"

She nodded her head. "I see that you resolved your differences with Elon yesterday."

Mark thought about the battle and the aftermath. "Actually, I think the Father resolved Elon's ego and anger management problems. You know what? He wants to talk to me about Yahshua sometime this week.

Sarah smiled and laid her head on Mark's shoulder. "That's good. I think you both needed him to do that."

Mark was about to reply when Charlie's voice spoke to them out of the air. "Mark, Sarah, to the War Room on the double."

Leaving their coffee cups, they jumped up and ran for the War Room. As they rushed in they saw that most of the Core Team was already there and getting into their places.

Jack motioned Mark over to his position. He looked at Mark, "It seems that our work with the Iranian "death ray" isn't over yet." Jack pointed at the big screen.

Mark looked at the screen and saw an almost identical set of patterns of swirls as he saw yesterday. He looked at Jack with a question on his face as David came into the War Room with eight Shield Generators in his hands.

Mark asked, "What, did I sleep all the way through a day? When did all this happen?"

Jack looked at the big digital clock at the bottom of the large screen. "About ten minutes ago. It seems that Major Abdullah's design had been replicated without his knowledge. The extras were probably prompted by the demons. According to Carol the Matrix indicates that they made six more of the devices before they lost the Major."

"Yesterday was their initial test with Nazari. Even though he never got to use it, apparently our response convinced them that we thought the thing would work. Now they have sent the other six devices over here to kill as many Israelis as possible."

Mark shook his head. "No, I don't think that is what happened. It takes way too much time to get just one of those things into Israel for them to have decided at the end of the battle yesterday to get the others in-country. This was part of the demon's plan all along. They didn't care if Nazari succeeded or not. They were just watching to see how we would respond. We found the right group of demons and we stopped them and Nazari. But, we just barely stopped them. They had already guessed that we don't have the resources to stop six at one time and now they know it."

Jack shook his head, "I believe that the Father knows that, too. That is why he released us to use the Force Generators in the up-coming battles."

Mark held up his hands, "Does that even matter? While we are stopping one group another group will use their device and could set off the ionized sky. We can't confront them all at once."

Jack looked Mark, "Mark, God knows this and yet he gave us permission to use the Generators and told us to stand forth against the enemy. I assume the enemy means the demons. God will handle the death rays."

Mark looked at Jack. "Okay then, it's a great plan, I'm glad to be a part of it. Suit up people, its back to work today." He stopped and asked Jack. "Umm, which one do you think we should stop first?"

Jack was about to answer when a new voice was heard from the doorway to the War Room. "You always attend to the closest one, of course. But, you're not going without me."

Mark looked over and saw Elon standing in the doorway with his battle armor on. Mark looked at Jack and quietly said, "He doesn't know about the Field Generators yet, does he?"

Jack whispered back as he got up to go to the Armory. "No, and they won't work for him, either."

CHAPTER SIXTEEN

This time there were five Ospreys warming up on the tarmac between the Mossad and the Crossfire sides of the Sea Base. Elon and the Core Team got on the first one. It lifted off when it was full. Charlie vectored them to the closest gathering of demonic activity. This time there was no time and energy wasted sneaking up on the demonic forces. The Osprey set down in the middle of the closest intersection and off loaded the troops. As it lifted off the next Osprey settled in to off load.

As the troops formed up Mark took Elon aside. He looked the man in the eyes. "No heroics needed this time. We have an ace up our sleeve that will let us take all the real demons down quickly. Unfortunately, I can't supply you with the same thing because it wouldn't work for you, yet. But, you can lead the IDF forces in shooting and killing every one of the uninvited and therefore illegal demons. Trust me on this, all right?"

Elon had made a decision yesterday to trust Mark so he said, "You do your thing and we'll see if there are any left for you to fight after we're done with them."

Mark shrugged his shoulders, "There are always more of them."

As the troops formed up there appeared on the street one demon. It was a mighty demon and there was supreme confidence on its face as it moved to attack the humans. Mark said, "Okay, where is the guy with the death ray gizmo?"

Jack shook his head. "I think this is a gigantic trap for us. I don't think that there are any duplicates of the death ray. That has to be an Archangel level demon. I think Satan is getting tired of feeding his lesser forces to the demon wood chipper, that would be us. Well, I believe in Yahveh and I haven't seen anything that tops these Generators as yet. Let's go send this large ugly character to the pit."

Mark thought that over. "Good plan, I think I'm glad I'm a part of it." He told Jack as he started to run at the demon. "I'll let you know in a minute."

Jack caught up with Mark, "You take him low and I'll take him high."

Mark asked Jack, "And what do the other eight people with us do?"

Jack felt that Holy Anger building in him again. "Tell them to pick any part they want." The Holy Anger was creating that overwhelming power within him again. "To Yahveh Elohim goes the victory!" He had the speed and he had the power and he leaped upward swinging his sword from his right to his left as Mark charged toward the beast's legs and went into the high-speed, time compression technique.

The two forces came together with a thunderous crash and Jack completed his initial slash as he collided with the huge demon. Mark took slice after slice out of the demon's legs and belly. Jack's force knocked the demon to the ground with Jack landing on its chest. Jack continued to stab, cut, and slash the upper part of the demon. His aggression exceeded his restraint as he also went into the time-compression mode and became the literal "whirling ball of blades" as he matched Mark and increased his stroke rate to twenty times more than normal.

Laura yelled at him "Jack, Stop!" Jack heard her and stopped attacking the demon which was almost completely dissolved into red smoke by then. Jack took a deep breath and told her. "Sorry, I was getting into that a little too much."

The Core Team walked back to the other troops and their swords and armor faded out. Jack looked back and saw that the rift had disappeared.

The Core Team switched off their Force Generators and stopped in front of the IDF forces. Elon stood there with his mouth open. He snapped it shut and asked, "What, how...how did you do that?" He was pointing out to the place in the street where there was a huge demon stain.

Mark just smiled. "When God doesn't like what Satan is doing he empowers us to stop the evil."

Elon shook his head, "Are you aware that before you turned that thing into Sushi he hit both of you two with those huge hammer fists of his that would have destroyed a tank? The shock waves from his blows were enough to knock us down all the way back here."

Jack looked at Mark, "Really? I didn't see that. I'll have to see Charlie's video of the battle." He answered his combat communicator and Charlie spoke. "Jack, I think your destruction of that upper level demon gave Satan a major upset stomach. It could only have been seen as an obvious warning from God. Satan has withdrawn all of the other groups. How are you going to explain the use of the Force Generators to Elon and his troops?"

Jack smiled, "I'm not going to mention them, Charlie. This was just an empowerment of Yahveh God that allowed us to defeat this demon. That is the truth without mentioning anything else. Okay, we're headed back to the base."

Charlie said, "Not so fast. We're directly in the sight pattern of several different satellites. Go destroy something else for the next ninety minutes."

Mark realized that the Israelis were keyed up to fight to the death but, didn't get to fire their weapons one time. They also could handle alcohol from what he had seen. This could be a good chance to release their pent-up energy and their intense disappointment. So, he cut into the conversation. "I say we take the boys here to a bar for a drink."

Jack couldn't believe Mark said that. Then he shook his head, "Why not."

CHAPTER SEVENTEEN

Several of the IDF troops knew of a local bar only a block away from where they were. He led the entire group over to the bar and caught the owner just opening up. "Could we have a drink at your establishment?" He asked of the man.

The older man looked out of his door and he saw over one hundred battle-hardened troops with weapons standing in front of his bar with three Ospreys standing behind them with their rotors turning and the machine guns in the side Portals pointing somewhat in his direction. Instead of fainting as he thought he ought to do he said, "Sure, why not, bar's empty right now and I have a bevy of pretty drink servers to take care of you."Sarah stepped up and told the man, "Then you'd better have some handsome men servers for us girls, too."

Jack thought the man won't know what to do with that request but he just nodded his head and started calling on his cell phone as the hundred troops filed into his bar. Jack thought that this was going to go down in the records for sure.

Later when they were back at the Sea Base Jack got a telephone call from the Prime Minister of Israel. "Jack, that battle was more than unbelievable, except that I have a dozen videos of it without the demon. I have dozens of personal accounts that the demon was huge and mighty. In the video you look like you're attacking the air except there was some kind of liquid splashing around and a great deal of red smoke."

Jack laughed, "We call the liquid "demon stain" and the smoke of the demon dissolving, "a good job". I'll have Charlie add in the demon for you and send a copy to you. It makes a lot more sense when you can visualize what we were fighting."

The Prime Minister thanked him and then cleared his throat, "Listen, Jack, about taking over one hundred armed troops to a bar. I have fielded a lot of complaints about that this morning."

Jack laughed, "Sorry Mr. Prime Minister, that was to take the edge off for the majority of the troops who were all geared up to fight the battle of their lives only to do nothing but stand by and watch. We did ask for and received permission from the owner before we entered. I personally paid the bar bill and gave the owner and the servers good tips. I will also cover any expenses or damages caused by the troops. We meant no disrespect; it just seemed like a good thing to do at the moment."

The Prime Minister laughed, "No, no, no, you don't understand, Jack. The complaints are from competing bars that felt left out of the party. Based on the owner and other accounts, your troops and our troops were model customers who left an additional serious tip that made the bar owner happy and popular. His bar has been jammed ever since then. On an official note I personally want to thank you and your team for stopping that demon before it could strike horror in the hearts of citizens all over Israel."

Jack thanked the PM and hung up. He gave the team an update and then turned back to Mark and Elon. "Sorry guys, I kind of had to take that call. Now, what do you two need?"

Mark leaned back in the chair he was in, "I want David, Alexis, Sarah, Laura, you, and me to get together with Elon and give him all the answers we have regarding his questions about Yahshua and Judaism. I think we owe him this and when I prayed about it I felt led to make sure it happens."

Jack looked at the two men for a few seconds while he prayed for God's will in the matter and the answer he got made him catch his breath. "Okay, no time like the present although I want to add Carol to the list. Let's see if everyone is available."

Jack knew that they would be available and the entire crew met in the conference room. After David, Alexis, Carol, Sarah, Laura, Mark, and Elon were seated comfortably, Jack asked if it was alright if he prayed for the success of the meeting. Everyone agreed and Jack bowed his head and muttered so that only Laura and Mark could hear what he said. "Hold onto your socks folks, God is going to run this show." Then he said louder, "Father Yahveh, we come before you in the name of your Son

Yahshua, in an attempt to resolve the questions and worries of your child, Elon Lukin, concerning your Kingdom."

Jack stopped praying and waited. The feeling of heaviness that he associated with the nearness of God's Holy Spirit continued to increase until all at once Jack sensed the approach of such purity and power he had to drop from his chair and prostrate himself on the floor. He felt the love of God flow through his body and he knew he was accepted. He rose and resumed his seat and was surprised to see everyone else doing the same thing. It had seemed to him that he had been on the floor all alone with the Lord.

Standing at the end of the table was a being of such power and purity that it was hard to look directly at him. Then the radiant glare softened until Jack saw a being that he knew was Yahshua standing at the end of the table. There was such a feeling of peace and love radiating from him that suddenly nothing else seemed important any more. Jack was content just to be in the presence of his Savior.

Yahshua looked at each of the people at the table and then he looked at Elon. A voice that vibrated in Jack's spirit said, *"Elon Lukin, you have wanted to know Me all your life but were afraid to go against the prevailing traditions of your people. Now, you have seen My Father reflected in these people and now you see Me. Your questions are not about your faith but about human laws. Know this, our Father and I look at the heart of a man and not at his physical being or his wealth or his words. Your heart is sorely troubled because of the thousands of years of human laws and teaching and your mandatory traditions. Speak to David and Sarah about this to find the answers to the questions you have. Our Father spoke through Laura during David's death and resurrection and through Sarah during the time of the poisoning of Yahveh's people in Israel and those of Jack's in America. Pray with your heart, not your mind and you will be free to accept Me. Look to Jack and Laura as you grow in your faith. They will lead you as you become a Mighty Warrior of Heaven."*

Yahshua looked at all of the people at the table. *"I bless you all for standing as righteous warriors for the*

Father's Kingdom. Your names are known in Heaven and your reward will be great, both in this life and the life to come. Peace I leave with you; My peace I give to you." Yahshua faded out of sight. Nobody moved or spoke for a while. Then Laura bowed her head and prayed their thankfulness to the loving God Yahveh for having His Son speak to them.

Elon was now buried in a deep conviction as he really concentrated on remembering every detail of the visitation. Jack quietly motioned for everyone except Sarah and Laura to get up and leave the room.

After he accepted the reality of every detail, he looked up and found only Sarah and Laura sitting with him. His tear-filled eyes touched Sarah's heart and she remembered that feeling was how she felt when David had been shot and killed and she knew it was Yahshua that brought him back to life. She smiled at Elon in camaraderie and asked him what he needed. Laura felt a powerful anointing on her to be a true representative of the living God. They began to talk about things great and small.

CHAPTER EIGHTEEN

Jack stared at the work he needed to finish laying on his desk in the War Room. Somehow it didn't seem important after the visit of the Savior. Something was unsettled in his spirit. He shut things down and went to his apartment. He found Laura sitting quietly in her favorite Bible study chair. He realized that this was the source of his unrest; he had needed to be here. There was contentment and a peace about Laura that attracted him like a flame draws a moth. He went into the bedroom and changed into soft casual clothing and grabbed his Bible and came back to where she quietly waited for him.

He ignored his lounger and sat down with his wife and suddenly wanted her closeness and her love. He stood up and drew her up next to him. He enfolded her in his arms and tenderly held her as close as he could. There was a love and sweetness there that he had been missing for some time. She nestled into his arms and rested in his strength and gentleness. She had a flash of memory of Jack in action this morning as he led the destruction of the large demon. The power and Holy Anger that fueled his assault on the creature was not to be denied. Yet, here he was, his arms as gentle as a dove's wings as he held her. She took in a deep breath and drew him down next to her on the couch.

He looked into her eyes and saw love and passion like golden sunlight radiating out of her spirit in a gentle fountain. He leaned down and kissed her on the lips. They held the kiss for a long time and they joyfully celebrated their overwhelming true and honest passion, love, and desire for each other.

A while later Laura breathed a gentle sigh and kissed the man she loved more than any other on the planet. She gently touched his face and said, "I still can't believe that God gave you to me." Jack laughed softly. "I think you have that backward. I'm the one that is blessed and I know it." She grinned, "I'm okay with that."

She was reflecting on the event that morning and said, "I was praying after seeing the Lord today. I understand now that you knew beforehand that He was going to be there, didn't you?"

Jack nodded, "Yeah, I got a word from the Father that His Son would be there if we prayed earnestly for Elon. I really didn't know what to expect but I knew it would be huge for everyone there, especially for Elon."

There was a happy glint in Laura's eyes. "I also noticed that the Lord told Elon to look to you and me for edification concerning Heavenly things on Earth. That is the first time those types of comments have included you, even putting you first. I am so very excited and happy to hear that. I know that the spiritual anointing flows from Heaven through Yahshua to the man of the family, the priest, and then to the woman and children. You have been a king your whole life and now you are the priest of this very large and royal family of warriors." She kissed him and held him in her arms and spoke a prayer of power and success over him.

Jack wasn't completely sure about his priesthood of the Crossfire Team but he also wasn't silly enough to argue with her, she was right a great deal of the time. He continued with the answer to her question of his knowing that Yahshua would be at the meeting this morning.

"God told me that Elon was a very special child of God and all Heaven was vibrating with anticipation of his learning the truth about Yahshua and becoming who he was anointed to be by God. Our living and eternal King also told me that He was proud that we, the team, showed Elon how one could walk in His balance of total love and Holy Anger. You know, none of this would have happened if we didn't continue to allow God to mold us into the people He wants us to be. I find it amazing that to a person, everyone on this team has forsaken their own desires and plans while willingly submitting their lives completely to Him as His anointed warriors. Yahshua was pleased with everyone on this team because we represent some the best that humanity can offer to their Elohim. Please understand that I am paraphrasing a bit here because He expressed all of this in four parallel concepts in one thought."

Laura let the tears of joy flow freely down her face as she heard the truth of God from her husband. She suddenly realized that she knew what he was saying was true because Hugo had told her these very things before during her training. The facts had been hidden in her mind until now. She looked at Jack and slid off the couch to kneel in a very humble thanksgiving to God. Jack joined her and they prayed together.

After a while Jack's prayers were stilled and shifted to a learning time for him. He realized he was excited by the teaching and fully committed to doing God's will in the coming battles.

Laura had snuggled into his embrace again and eventually fell asleep in his arms. Jack looked at the peace on her pretty face and he silently thanked God for giving them this time together. He thought back to when they first found God in what had seemed as the darkest days of their pampered lives. Hah! If he had even remotely suspected at that time what the future held for them both he wouldn't have believed it.

He leaned down and gently kissed Laura on the forehead. She smiled in her sleep. He pulled his knees under him and then lifted her carefully and took her to the bed. He tucked her in, turned the lights down, and quietly left to let her sleep. He realized that he had things he needed to do for God that were suddenly very important.

CHAPTER NINETEEN

Jack found the War Room still empty with nothing showing on the Action Board. As he sat down he realized that he was about to change that in a big way. The vision that he had received from the Father was troubling but it was commanded by God that the team respond.

As he prayed for guidance and protection from any demonic eavesdropping in any of their actions he began to understand the direction that God wanted the team to go this time. He realized, from a human view, that the commanded actions seemed quite overwhelming and completely hopeless in the extreme. He keyed his microphone and asked Carol to come to the War Room. As he waited for her to show up he called Charlie Wu.

Linda Wu answered his call and asked what was needed. Jack thought, "Boy, this woman is direct. No chit-chat, not a word of social interaction on any level. But he had to admit to himself that she was highly effective in their world."

Jack smiled, knowing how that changed the sound of the human voice, "Hello Linda. Is Charlie available at the moment?"

"No, he isn't. Can I help you or would you like him to call you when he is available?"

Jack thought about that for a few seconds. "I would like both of you to come to the War Room and discuss a mission with me. I believe that it will take both of you to reason this out."

"I will find out when Charlie is available. Just a second."

There were a few seconds of silence and then Charlie came on the line. "Hi, Jack. I understand that you need Linda and I in the War Room. We'll be right down."

Jack smiled, "I'll see you then." As he hung up the connection he suddenly was able to see the huge responsibility that was on the Wu's backs. Not only did they oversee all the communication, planning, and defense of the team around the world. But they also were responsible for the security of the Sea Base and all the part time personnel for the team, plus now; both being active in combat as sword bearers. He realized that the team had grown greatly but he had not considered the increasing load he was placing on the two ex-spies.

The two Asians came through the door of the War Room at that point. Jack indicated that they should all sit at a small conference table rather than their work station positions. He studied them both for a few seconds letting his experience as a business manager lead him in his thoughts.

"Charlie, will you and Linda step out of your roles for a few minutes and be straight with me as to the amount of stress the team operations are putting on you these days?"

Charlie's expression didn't change nor did his wife's countenance show any emotion at Jack's question. But, Jack could almost see the wheels turning in their minds. Charlie looked at his wife for a few seconds and then turned to Jack.

"I'm glad you initiated this conversation Jack. The load has gotten to a point where it is starting to adversely affect both of us. I was going to seek you out about this as soon as the action let up. That's part of the problem. The action is not letting up, it is constantly becoming more demanding on the COMSEC resources and there are no breaks to allow us to make adjustments. The stress is becoming exponential and quickly leading to a level that is more than we can absorb. Both Linda and I have been praying for direction from the Father. The only fruitful leading I have received is to bring it to you and the rest of the leadership for some kind of resolution. It is not in either of our natures to give up or to complain about the greatest opportunity we've ever had."

Jack nodded, "The Father put this problem on my heart today, also. Maybe we need to do what God told Moses to do in the desert in Numbers 11:16."

Jack called it up on his tablet. *"The Lord said to Moses: "Bring me seventy of Israel's elders who are known to you as leaders and officials among the people. Have them come to the tent of meeting that they may stand there with you. I will come down and speak with you there, and I will take some of the power of the Spirit that is on you and put it on them. They will share the burden of the people with you so that you will not have to carry it alone."*

Jack smiled at his two friends, "I don't think we need seventy people because we're not leading several million people. But I realize it is past time to delegate the day-to-day operations of the COMSEC department to trustworthy people so that you two can be released to do things more along the lines of which you both are so talented. I will expect you both will want to maintain the control over the high level choices and development issues for COMSEC. But, the leading I got from the Father today is that you are needed as active components of the Core Team.

Jack reached over and took one of Linda's hands and one of Charlie's hands. "I apologize for taking this long to get involved, but you guys do such a good job and never complain, yet you both are completely indispensable to the team's operation every minute of every day. We could not do what we do without your efforts and the whole team knows that. Who are your most talented staff members?"

Charlie breathed a big sigh of relief. "Thank you. This has been building on my heart for weeks. I take it to the Lord in prayer and He tells me to wait. But, there is a problem. Of all the talented people I have working in COMSEC; there is no one that can do the job that I Linda and I are doing. Not because they aren't computer smart and dedicated. They all are in it for the long haul and always give their all in fulfilling a mission."

"The problem is that none of the Christians I have employed have the necessary background or capability to be leaders with a vision of the future. They are great workers but they need direction instead of being able to give it. Since Ethan went to the Core Team my most probable choice is a Hindu. I just don't have anyone I can honestly promote, with any confidence, that it will be God's choice or that they can do the job."

Jack nodded, "I believe that we need to ask God to find the person He wants in that position. Based on past performance I'll be surprised if the person we need isn't already involved with us in some way."

CHAPTER TWENTY

Jack looked at Linda and asked, "Okay, for the team effort now, how about you Linda? What do you really need?"

Linda stared at Jack so long he thought that she wasn't going to say anything. He was about to make a suggestion when she spoke. She looked at Charlie first, "Thank you, Jack, for considering me and my life. I dearly love my husband and what we are doing for the team and the Lord. I truly love it more than anything that is material or business related. I was very excited and pleased when I was a part of the mission to Russia with the other women of the team. I feel lately that I am considerably isolated while being useful and helpful in supporting the COMSEC group. I long for more of the excitement that I get every time Charlie and I are involved in field operations. That is what I long for but cannot do while Charlie and I are so intertwined in the day-to-day operations in COMSEC."

Charlie's face showed that he grudgingly agreed with Linda and her inability to interact with the other women of the team.

Jack thought over everything they had discussed and said, "Let's pray and see if our Heavenly Father will resolve these issues for us. I apologize because I didn't see these problems until now and I want you both to know that we value your part in the team but more so because we value you as friends."

Laura walked into the room and stopped in the doorway when she saw the discussion in progress. She was bumped into the room by Carol who was coming in right behind Laura when she stopped suddenly.

Jack grinned and waved them both over to the table. "You are just in time to help pray for a new leader for the COMSEC group to work under the Wu's and handle the daily operations of the group.

Laura and Carol sat down at the table. Laura leaned close to Charlie and Linda. "You had better brace yourselves. The last time Jack prayed today, Yahshua himself walked into the room."

Jack raised an eyebrow at Laura as if to say. "Really? I heard that. I'm sure that my prayers are no more effective than anybody else."

Jack felt an unusual leading and had the five people around the table hold hands in a circle. "Heavenly Father, Creator of the Universe and Eternal King of Kings. We praise Your mighty name and ask humbly in Your Son's name, for guidance in the matter of filling the position of a bold leader for the Communications and Security Section of Your Crossfire Team. Father, we ask that the person You send to us is a man or woman of God and faithful and true to Your Commandments and the duties of that position. We know that you know the beginning and the end of all things and our plea asks for such a person that stands on Your Word until the end. We ask this in Yahshua's name, Amen"

Jack stood up and the others rose, also. Jack felt led to put one of his hands on the heads of both Linda and Charlie. As he prayed his blessings on both of them he noticed that the prayer seemed to be a living thing that created energy waves in the air around both of them. He continued to pray "Father, bless both of these people and their lives in service to You. Then he was led to add, "Father, bless these two believers with the desires of their hearts and make them mighty warriors for You for the rest of eternity. We pray all of this in Yahshua's name, Amen."

Both Charlie and Linda looked up and stared at Jack. He had never seen either one of the classical Chinese types look amazed. He looked from one to the other, "What?"

Laura answered for them. "Your face is glowing with the presence of God."

Charlie and Linda thanked him and left for COMSEC. Jack turned to Carol. He smiled and asked her if she would study the Matrix for relationships between the Crossfire Team and the realm of Hell as it concerned an imminent mission for the team.

Carol studied Jack for a few seconds. She leaned over and tentatively reached out with her hand and touched his face. Her eyes rolled up and she crumpled backward and sort of melted to the floor so quickly Laura couldn't catch her. Laura knelt down and cradled Carol's head in her lap.

Jack got up and walked out of the War Room. He went to the Restroom on the first floor. Shoving the door open a little too hard, it banged off the wall. He walked over to a sink and looked at his image in the mirror. He could see the golden glow that his face had. He reached up and touched it. Nothing happened. He prayed. "Heavenly Father, please reveal the meaning of this glow on my face."

He immediately heard the Father say, *"Jack, you are My anointed to pray for your people and I am with you as you pray. You are only reflecting My glory in truth and honesty. You are transferring My love to those you pray for in My Son's name. You are affected by My power flowing through you."*

Even though he didn't completely understand the change in his prayers, he dropped to his knees and prayed for forgiveness for his sin of lack of understanding and thanked the Father for the newness in his life."

Returning to the War Room he was much more composed than when he had left. He found Carol sitting at the table with a glass of water that Laura had gotten her.

She closed her eyes and remembered the purity and power of God she had felt when she touched the glow on Jack's face. It had overwhelmed her and she had passed out. She looked up at Jack. She smiled a small smile "Forgive me for acting so inappropriately. I could feel the presence of the Lord in the glow on your face and wanted. . . I don't know. I guess I wanted to see what it felt like."

Jack looked at the young lady that was wise beyond her years. "Carol, you were right to want to touch the power of God, we all want to do that. Also, there is no sin involved because your body responded to that power. Be filled with the peace and the love of God and know He reached out to touch you, too."

Carol's eyes shone at Jack's words. She shook her head to help remind her of why she was there and what Jack had asked her to do. Then she remembered that she had been determining the correctness of the leading she had received three days ago. She asked the Father if what she was going to tell Jack was His will.

Sensing approval from God she spoke carefully. "Jack, God put that same request about the team and Hell on my heart several days ago and I believe He is now allowing me to give you the answer."

Carol was precise in what she said, "What I have seen in the Matrix frightens me, but my anointing requires that I speak out what the Father wants me to speak. Soon a select group of the Crossfire Team will attack the demonic realm itself. This is to fulfill God's righteousness and to bring to a complete halt one of Satan's most evil and illegal efforts ever against mankind. God has strictly forbidden the demonic to do anything like this. We have to understand that this action by the enemy of man is so egregious that God will not permit it even though it directly concerns Satan himself."

Carol looked into Jack's eyes." You are aware that the team has no license or right to directly damage or attempt to destroy Satan himself because his fate has been determined and prophesied by God and the team does not have any part in that fate. But, God is going to use the team to destroy any and all of Satan's demons and the domain that relates to this effort to make it clear to Satan that enough is enough."

"God is going to use us to make it crystal clear to Satan, that if he doesn't stop his escalation of these heinous and unapproved schemes, that God will take a great part of his power away from him to do anything but what has been prophesied, until the end of the thousand-year reign of His Son on Earth. This is the message God wants the team to deliver to Satan by clearly destroying absolutely everything associated with this latest scheme."

Jack and Laura sat there dumbfounded. Laura thought back to when she was required to get into a jet fighter and fly from Houston, Texas to Greece in five hours. She was just days away from having been nothing more than a housewife and financial adviser with absolutely no background as a warrior.

She fell back on her strength and prayed almost tearfully for God's peace and assurance that she could do this thing. She thought, "This was huge even in the life they were now living. Directly going against Satan himself? How could she face that level of evil and do God's will?"

Jack felt that bottomless pit yawning below him again as he had in the Men's clothing store in Denver when God called him to be more than he was. "Well, this was a LOT more than he was."

Carol felt even more worried that she would not be able to do her part in this mission. She felt that the Father might need her to go with the others of the team on this mission and she couldn't even conceive of the spiritual forces involved on both sides and the power of the Universe that was about to be unleashed.

Mark picked this time to walk into the War Room and ask, "Hi guys, what's up?

CHAPTER TWENTY-ONE

Jack looked at his best friend in the world. He shook his head and said, "I think we need a bigger boat."

Mark recognized actor Roy Schneider's line from the "Jaws" movie of 1975 after his character had seen the size of the shark they were trying to kill. As Mark remembered it, the shark was bigger than the boat they were on. Exactly how this applied to the Crossfire Team he wasn't sure.

Two minutes later he knew how it applied and he wasn't sure now that he wanted to know. "I assume that this isn't a mission we can refuse?"

Laura laughed, "It has been assigned to us by God and I don't believe there is a back door for this mission any more than there was one for the people at the Alamo. If there was you'd have to run really fast just to catch up to me."

Jack looked at Mark. "If we are successful in this mission, do you think it will bring us up on Satan's radar even more than we are already?"

Mark shook his head, "How bad do you think he'll make it for us if we take this mission and fail it?"

Laura looked at Carol, "Did you get the list of personnel that are to go on this mission?"

Carol shook her head. "All I got was that it would be a "select group of the Crossfire Team"."

Mark stood up. "All right, enough of the chit-chat. Let's start planning this walk in the park as if the entire Crossfire Team is going to go and then adapt and overcome any changes. First thing I have a question about is this. Other than living really badly and dying poorly, just how does one get to Hell?"

Laura had seen a small blink of brilliant white and gold and she responded, "Let's ask someone who knows the spiritual dimension better than we do."She looked up and said "Well, Rose, how do we get to Hell?"

There was a swirl of gold and white and the angel Rose appeared in the middle of the War Room. She looked at the five people present and settled on Laura. "To get to the realm of the demons that you call Hell you have to have access to that spiritual dimension. Since the Most High is sending you to confront Satan, I believe He will transport you to where He wants you to go."

Mark quipped, "Is that a round trip or a one-way package?"

Rose looked at Mark. "That will depend entirely upon you, Mark, and the team's success or failure on the mission."

Jack sighed again. "Rose, can you tell us the rules of engagement or even the reason we are going there?"

Rose frowned. "That has not been given to me to share with you. The Most High will give you that information when He is ready, I am sure."

Laura asked the angel, "Do you know the names of the select group of the Crossfire Team that will go?"

The angel nodded her head. "Yes, which I do know and can tell you. The team going to confront Satan includes Mark and Sarah, David and Alexis, Charlie and Linda, Megan, Sean, and one half of the Sensitive Operations Group. The other Core Team members and remaining SOG will face the challenges here in the human world while the away team is, well, away."

Jack studied the angel carefully. "May I ask why my wife and I are being excluded from the trip to Hell?"

Rose turned to Jack and approached him. When she was within a foot or so she reached out and placed her left hand against Jack's chest. "As of your visitation today, Yahshua anointed you as the Priest or Spiritual Leader of the Crossfire Team." A pulse of intensely solid white power came from Rose's hand and slammed into Jack's chest and then spread throughout his body.

Jack sensed the same empowerment he had experienced in the last several battles with major demons. White power was filling him up with what felt like unlimited energy and the desire to conquer anything for Heaven. The power seemed to soak through Jack's whole being and everyone except Laura stepped back from the white power pulsing from Jack's body. Laura was attracted to the power.

Rose circled around Jack and then held her left hand above his head and her right hand above his heart. "As the

Priest or Spiritual Leader anointed by the Son of God "your prayers are now *the effectual fervent prayers of a righteous man and as such they will avail much for the team.*" I urge you to use this power with all due respect for and in honor to the Most High."

"Your prayers are needed by all the members of the team. It is important that you anoint Mark as the Priest or Spiritual Leader for the people going with him. I can tell you that your prayer coverage for them while they are away will be critical to the success of their mission."Jack's white glow had settled down but it didn't completely disappear.

The beautiful angel floated over to Laura. Rose placed her hand on Laura's chest and the power flashed again. Rose circled Laura and covered her head and her heart as she had done for Jack. "Laura, as Yahveh said, you and your husband are one flesh and therefore you share his anointing for priestly or spiritual leadership. As Yahshua treated women with equality in His time, your place is to stand by your husband's side as an equal in power for the people. Your heart will now lead you truly and your prayers will be powerful to the glory of God the Father. Jack will need your support and guidance. I can tell you that all Heaven is so proud of you, warrior woman."

Jack asked Rose, "Why do you refer to "a demonic realm" rather than the name "Hell"?"

Rose smiled at Jack. "That is because neither Heaven nor Hell is a part of mankind's reality yet. The people that have passed beyond the boundary of life are waiting to be judged at the end of the age before they go to their reward. They will sense no time passing during their wait. It will seem to them that the instant they leave this life they will stand before God."

"The first beings to suffer the second death which is the Lake of Fire or "Hell," are the Anti-Christ and the False Prophet. This will occur when the Son of God returns to the Earth. They will be tortured day and night for a thousand years before the holy Angels and the Lamb. After that there will be the Great White Throne Judgment."

"At that time Satan and all those that serve him, along with all those who do not accept the Son of God as their

Lord and Savior are sent to the Lake of Fire. At that time Heaven will become real for the faithful in God."

Mark asked Rose, "I don't understand. If the devil and his followers, which would include the demons, are to be tortured in Hell, who is going to torture them or anybody else who goes to Hell?"

Rose quoted from Revelation 14:12 "*they, too, will drink the wine of God's fury, which has been poured full strength into the cup of His wrath. They will be tormented with burning sulfur in the presence of the holy angels and of the Lamb*" Mark's realized the truth about the reality of the punishment of sin.

Rose smiled at everyone and blessed them all in the Name of the Most High, Yahveh as she swirled out of sight in a blaze of solid gold and flaming white.

Jack walked over to Mark who rose to meet him. Jack frowned, "I don't like this and I don't want to go along with it. We've been a team since the beginning and I do not want to leave you and the others to face Satan and the demonic region without me. I feel this makes me out to be a person who lacks the courage to endure dangerous things and I don't really want to stay here in safety while you go in harm's way."

Mark grabbed Jack and hugged him. Then, holding him at arm's length he smiled, "Well, buddy, I would switch with you in a New York second, but it looks like it's my turn to shine on the road to Hell and back. Yes, I know it really isn't Hell yet. That's okay; I'm going to call it Hell, anyway. But, remember this. I don't hold anything against you for not being there. I will miss you and Laura more than you know. But, you and I don't have a choice. If God says for you to stay here and He's arranging the transportation, you aren't going to go regardless of what you or I want."

Seeing the look on Jack's face Mark smiled again. "It's okay, I've got this. I also figured out how we can still fight the enemy together in the future. Just take the whole team. Rose says that you have to be available for all the team members. So..."

The other people who had come in to see what was happening, left the War Room talking excitedly and went to tell others about what just happened.

Jack turned to Laura and saw nothing but love and pride in his anointing. He wrapped his arms around her. "Well, love of my life, what do you think about all this?"

Laura grinned, "I am also unhappy that they have to go in harm's way while we stay here in safety. But, the Father makes the rules and we gave our lives and our complete obedience to Him." She smiled a little and quietly asked, "Do you think that we can maintain a functional relationship as man and wife now that you are the Priest of the team as well as the home?"

Jack noticed the glint in her eye. "Remember, Priests of the Old Testament fathered many children. Also, God told you through Rose that you will be the mother of great warriors for Him. Well, I think that implies there needs to be a father, too."

She laughed, "Yes, but remember how Mary gave birth to Yahshua?"

Jack got down on one knee and looked up at his beautiful wife. "Will you marry me, again? I want us to be together as one forever."

Laura laughed again; she turned around and sat on his knee. She touched his nose with her finger. "Too late buster, you're already mine for eternity and I think one eternity should be enough to get you trained."

Jack asked "Is there a carrot and stick involved in this "training"?"

She said "definitely". Then she got up and pulled Jack up. "Come on, just because you went and got all righteous doesn't mean you get out of helping to plan this mission."

CHAPTER TWENTY-TWO

Jack sat on one of the sofas in the living area of the Sea Base in prayer. His prayer was that God would give them a plan for the assault on Hell. He was amazed when he heard from the Father before he even finished his prayer.

"My son, I am giving you all the information for the assault and what I command concerning this despicable thing that Satan has commanded. Destroy them completely. Their sickness will easily spread if it isn't eradicated to the last atom. My angels will be with the team as will I."

Jack prayed his thanks to God and got up and went to find Mark and Sarah. As he came into the War Room Sarah was just heading out for something and as Jack walked into the room she grinned and curtseyed bending her knee and bowing.

Jack narrowed his eyes at her and raised an eyebrow. "You looking for a lecture young woman?" Sarah hung her head and said, "On no, great one."

Jack grinned at Mark as Sarah ran out of the room. "You need to get your woman in line, mister."

Mark looked up at Jack, "Would you try doing that? Please, I failed miserably when I tried it. Do you know that woman carries a hide-out gun even when she is in a bikini? No! I am not going to try again to get her in line because I'm too young to die."

By this time everyone in the War Room, including Jack and Laura, were laughing hard enough to cry.

Jack took Mark over to the conference table behind the work stations, sat him down, and pushed a pad of paper at him." I just got a download from the Father on the mission to Hell. I'll tell you what I got and you write it down, okay?"

Twenty minutes later they had six pages with writing on both sides. Jack took the sheets over to the computer printer. He scanned both sides of them into the computer. He then had Charlie turn them into a spreadsheet on the big screen.

Sarah read the first page of the notes and turned to Mark, "That's the foulest, most despicably evil thing I have ever heard of in the Universe! I cannot wait to kill every demon that wants to make this repulsive operation a reality."

Jack just nodded his head in agreement. He knew what it said. Mark just sat there with his jaw clenched. Laura read the words on the screen with trepidation.

"I am the Lord your God. I have called the fire god Moloch detestable for millennia. My words command that you shall not pass your children through the fire to this detestable false god. This deceitful worship is now being changed into such a terrible sin against Me, that I will no longer tolerate him or his disobedience."

"Satan's demons have used subtle intimidation and sought to control minds night and day and are now ready to achieve Moloch's goal. Now that the groundwork has been done around the world, thousands of Moloch's demons have been prepared by Moloch to kill and replace the leaders of the Zultarian religion at all levels throughout the world. This is being done in direct defiance of My commandment that demons are not to enter the human world and become human. Satan has determined that he will allow Moloch to do this thing. To achieve Moloch's goals, Satan has reasoned in his mind that it is acceptable to defy Me and is daring Me to stop him. This will not be allowed to happen."

"These thousands of demonic replacements, at every level, will seduce the followers of that useless idol religion so that the only solution to make the rest of the world subservient to their false religion is in the total obedience to the worship of Moloch"

"In true demonic fashion the children they will sacrifice to this detestable false god are not their own children who are exempt. But all children in all of the lands they have conquered or suborned by passive invasion. One billion innocent young children and infants are to be destroyed in Moloch's fire, their screams and cries of pain blotted out by drums and loud music as the leaders of their nations cheer a better world. Then, when all of the children of the oppressed have been offered up to Moloch, then the demons will force the Zultarians to sacrifice their children, also."

"I, the Lord your God, will not allow this evil to happen. I command you to go to the demonic realm to prevent this from happening. If you destroy the demons before they can become a force on Earth over the Zultarian people, I will allow a great resurgence of moral understanding and righteous anger by parents the world over and they will wrest the lives of their children back from the cult of Moloch and to drive out the evil doers in their governments that support this despicable false god."

"I will take you and your team to the kingdom of Moloch's demons so that you can execute My sentence on all of them and on Moloch himself. There are twelve thousand demons that serve him and have been prepared to enter your world in three days. I will ensure that none of them can escape My wrath that is you." Destroy them all to the last atom. This sickness must stop now. I will cause plans of the small realm that you are to destroy, to appear on your computers. I cannot grant you the use of the Force Generators because this is your attack and not in defense against an illegal attack by the demons. But, you may use any form of weapons you chose to excise this evil from the demonic kingdom totally. I will fill all of you, My warriors, with righteous anger and give you the vision to end this. I, the Lord your God have spoken. In two days I will send you as a wave of My all-consuming fire."

CHAPTER TWENTY-THREE

Mark and Charlie studied the plans of the demonic realm of Moloch and attempted to develop a plan of attack that would be effective and at the same time efficient.

Mark shook his head, "I've got twenty-five warriors and twelve thousand demons. If we use the sword to destroy that entire group that means each person needs to destroy roughly four hundred and eighty demons. If everyone can destroy two demons per minute, that will mean everyone has to kill demons non-stop for four hours." Mark looked perplexed. "I don't think I could do that."

Charlie asked him, "Since you are going to be in their domain and not here on Earth what can we kill them with other than the swords?"

Charlie's wife, Linda, had previously entered the office to update satellite data and load it onto the massive solid state memory banks that could only be accessed from Charlie's office. She had been listening to the discussion and suddenly rolled her chair over to the table the men were working at.

"I think I have an idea that could improve our odds greatly."

Mark looked at her with expectant hope."How do we do that?"

Linda gently shooed Charlie away from his desk and started typing a search code that brought up the after-action reports. She selected the one that Debbie Hargrove had written in Russia the day that she had killed Sam Sturgis. Linda ran another short search and found the entries she was looking for. She selected the important ones and brought them up on one of the large screens above Charlie's desk. The three of them read the report section carefully.

"As I ran I got a leading or at least an unusual thought. I was led to remove the magazine from the rifle and using only one hand, I removed the rounds out of the magazine. When I had them all out, I held them in my hand and prayed, *"Father, I ask You to bless these bullets in Your mighty name so that they will do Your Will against the enemies of all mankind. Make these bullets an extension of Your will and Esteem. Guide them in Your Will and bless the work they do against the enemy."*

I had trouble reloading them as it was more complicated but I managed to reload the magazine and reinsert it by the time I reached the top of the hill. I ran to the far side of the flat section and dropped to my knees.

I found a convenient mound of rock and I adjusted the fixed 10-power sniper scope and scanned the road where it came back uphill about a thousand yards from the hilltop. I did not see anything on the road. Using the bolt, I loaded the first round into the chamber. I took a deep breath and patiently scanned the road again. All at once the motor scooter with Sam Sturgis appeared, heading away from the town.

I took a medium breath and steadied my sights. I had already sighted the scope in for the maximum range. I then prayed that the Father would bless the work of my hands. I took up the slack in the trigger, sighted on the back of Sam's head, led the target due to his speed, exhaled half of my breath and squeezed the trigger. I quickly cycled the bolt and repeated the operation but a little lower. I got off three shots before the first one got to the target.

My mind played over two things that startled me this time. The first was that I could actually see the bullets in flight. They weren't like normal lead or copper bullets; they were glaringly white hot with an incandescent center that had the same esteem rolling off of them I had seen on Laura's sword. They were running true and straight toward the target when I half saw a demon try to deflect the rounds. The first round went through the demon's hand and blew him away. That round impacted on the back of Sam Sturgis' neck terminating his life. The other two insurance rounds impacted on the headless body throwing it off the scooter and into the ditch at the side of the road.

Mark said, "Wow, I think that would work! I'm really glad your memory is so sharp, Linda. I have to find Jack and Laura. I wonder if that would work with grenades and man-pad missiles too."

Charlie asked, "Do you think that would work in the demon's dimension? I mean, we don't know if that demon she "blew away" with one of the bullets was legally in our dimension or an illegal."

Mark smiled at Charlie, "Not to worry partner, the power she prayed for on those bullets would have killed the demon in either case. Also, God is the author and creator of all things. That will include the demonic realm. I will bet you breakfast in bed for a week it'll work,"

Mark rushed out of the COMSEC office to find the Malones. Charlie shook his head and said to Linda. "That guy plays all the angles. If this idea doesn't work, we probably won't make it back to have breakfast."

CHAPTER TWENTY-FOUR

Jack realized that he was beginning to think like Laura. As soon as Mark explained what Linda had shown them and Jack wanted to see what he thought, he said, "Let's pray about it."

They bowed their heads and Jack prayed, "Father Yahveh, cleanse us in your Holy Name's sake. We praise your Holy Name Yahveh and exalt your presence. All glory and honor is yours Abba. In Yahshua's name we come humbly before you to seek an answer to Mark's concern of how to do Your Will in the matter of the attack on Satan's domain. We pray for Your glory on the bullets, grenades, missiles and other weapons to allow us to destroy the overwhelming number of demons rather than killing them one at a time with Your sword of Esteem."

They fell quiet and waited on the Lord for edification. Nothing happened, no angels, no words, simply silence. Jack wondered if he had presented the problem correctly or not.

Laura came over and stood by the table. Jack looked at her and nodded. She handed him a piece of paper. Unfolding it Jack read it twice and shook his head as he grinned. He stood up and told Mark to go with him.

They went down to the Armory. Jack walked in and asked the SOG warrior manning the Armory, "You have a pallet load for me?"

Sergeant Howell nodded his head. "Problem is Sir, there is no paperwork, no bill of lading, and I didn't see anyone deliver it through the security system."

Jack had an idea what it was. "That's okay, Sergeant. I'll sign for it. Where is it?"

The Sergeant turned around and pointed at a crate about eight feet tall and six foot on either side, not ten feet away from them. Jack took a clipboard and filled out the bill of lading and signed it "*as received*."

Mark had walked over and couldn't find any markings or labels on the massive crate. Jack handed him a pry bar and the two of them pried off the end of the crate. Inside were eight more crates. As they opened those crates Mark got more and more excited. There were thousands of rounds of 6.8 mm ammo, hundreds of rifle fired grenades and even six shoulder mounted LAW missiles with launchers.

Jack took one of the bullets out of a magazine and looked at the business end of the round. At the front end of the round was a glowing crystal-like tip that looked the same to Jack as the point of the spears he had been given by God to destroy two major demons.

Mark looked at the bullet and slapped Jack on the back. "Laura said your prayers were powerful but I never expected this."

Jack put the bullet back into the magazine. "Funny thing is; I did expect something like this."

Jack had Sergeant Howell put all of the contents of the crate into a special secured room and locked it out of sight and out of reach until the team left for their road trip to Hell. "Sergeant, I want you to take special care of this shipment. It is the equalizer for the road trip troops and we don't want anything to happen to it."

The Sergeant smiled, "Don't worry Sirs; I'm part of the road trip troops. That order couldn't be safer than if it was a baby in its mother's arms.

Back in the War Room Jack went over Mark's plan which was pretty much his normal plan of "go there, kill everything, and leave". The only difference this time was the number of enemy that needed to go to the pit. Mark had set up an interesting sequence of destruction for the Earth bound demons that worked for Moloch. Jack noticed that Mark had assigned Moloch to himself and Sarah. Nothing new about that except he had set them up to face the eternal old evil before the rest of the troops attacked the mass of demons.

Jack asked him about the wisdom of doing that. Mark smiled at him and said. "You know, cut the head off the snake and the body dies."

Jack snorted, "That didn't work too well in the movie Sahara, did it?"

Mark grinned, "I plan to apply a lot more finesse to the program than Dirk Pitt did."

Jack stared at Mark. "You know that what you're going up against is not humorous, right?"

Mark sat back in his chair and looked off into the future. "Yes, I know that nothing about this is funny, it's as serious as a heart attack. But, if I don't joke about it, the seriousness wins and that's not uplifting no matter how you look at it. We are going in there tomorrow with limited Intel and no satellite oversight. We think the ammo and grenades and missiles will work to cut down the numbers, but we've never done anything like this and we just don't have any previous experience. No one I've ever met went to Hell and came back. I have my wife's life and twenty-three others in my hands and if I make a mistake there may be no happy future of any of us. I would be scared but my prayers say that our God is taking us to it and He will take us through it."

Jack put his arm on Mark's shoulder and told him. "I really do have every confidence in you and your ability. I trust you and do not doubt you."

Mark smiled, "Well, I sure hope you are right."

CHAPTER TWENTY-FIVE

Mark went to make sure that everyone on the Away Team was prepared and had been issued the "special" ammo, grenades, and missiles.

Sarah laid out the contents of her combat backpack, hip pack and chest pack. "Does this meet the Commander's requirements for each of us?"

Mark carefully checked the emergency supplies, water, energy bars, flash lights, Night Vision Goggles, gloves, knives, guns, backup gun, and flares. Then he checked the bandolier of replacement magazines for the M-8 rifles and the handguns. Other clandestine and spy stuff and the most important item, two collapsed rolls of toilet paper. "Check, check."

Mark inspected his packs and then sat down on the bed and lifted the thing that had been a major surprise in the ammo crate. He lifted the spear, carefully watching the fabric of reality swirl and bend at the crystal tip. Jack had told him what it was for and Mark had nodded. "I saw you use the one on the demon in Germany. It was very effective and I believe that this one will also be effective."

Mark hefted the spear and prayed, "Father Yahveh, cover this spear with your power and your love and give it the full truth of your word for Moloch." Mark felt a vibration go through the spear and the tip glowed. Then the spear shimmered out of sight. Mark knew without a doubt that it would appear when he needed it.

Back in the War Room, Charlie Wu walked over to Jack. "You have a minute to talk to me?"

Jack looked up at him and nodded. "You want to meet here or elsewhere?"

Charlie indicated that they should go out into the large living area. The two men walked into the spacious room and went over to the circle of seats, part way into the living area to separate themselves from some of the Away Team that was having a last bite to eat in the dining area.

Charlie sat down and smiled at Jack. "I believe that I have arrived at a solution for all of the problems we discussed with the COMSEC Department."

Jack thought about that. He hadn't been able to identify any one to replace Charlie and Linda's operational roles so far. "I'm all ears Charlie, who are we talking about?"

Charlie smiled again. "I was praying for a solution when God dropped a clever solution in my mind. I am going to replace my role and that of my wife with my version of a cyborg.

Jack stared at Charlie trying to see what he was proposing. "Go on, spell it out for me."

Charlie nodded his head. "I propose we promote Ethan Reaper to the position of Manager of the COMSEC Department. I know that Ethan doesn't have my level of knowledge in areas such as spy craft, spy Intel or experience. In one sense that makes him an ideal candidate for this job. He's like a fresh piece of paper for us to write on and he doesn't have to unlearn a lot of faulty knowledge or history. But, on his side he has a superb anointing for computers and software. Plus, there is his innate intelligence and his youth. Now, to give him the edge on all the things he doesn't have yet, I propose we make Crayton a mandatory resource for the Manager's position."

Charlie looked to see if Jack was still listening to him or if he had decided to forget this probability. Jack was still listening intently and apparently interested in this concept.

"Crayton has been a functioning intelligence for this team for the last three years. I have repeatedly improved his software to the point I don't have anything left I can do to improve his mental processes. You see, Crayton has all of my cautions, worries, and knowledge. I think he has been my alter-ego for so long I think he is taking on my characteristics as the easiest way to achieve the results I want."

"I have spent the last twenty-four hours upgrading and integrating Crayton into the actual daily operations for the department and he is almost good enough to run things on his own, but he needs someone to refine his tactics and approve his findings, and input new problems. I think

Ethan will be the perfect human input for Crayton's operational skills. The only concern I have is that I may be creating something I can't top for operational superiority for the team."

Charlie stopped talking and stared at Jack. Jack was praying and looking for any possible drawbacks or dangers in letting a "cyborg" union run the department. Actually he felt that Charlie had come up with an extremely good answer to the problem. He felt that the Father agreed with that summation. He looked at Charlie, "Do you feel we could get this "union" functioning before you take your vacation to Hell?"

Charlie nodded. "At least I can assure you that the Crayton persona is ready. I will leave Mr. Reaper to you to break the news to him. I believe that the Father is for this union. Let me know when the three of us can talk, but it needs to be soon. I still have a bunch of things like passwords and authorizations I need to pass over to him before he can function in that position."

Jack keyed his microphone and called Ethan. He answered on the second ring. He sounded out of breath and Jack asked him what he was doing.

Ethan sighed, "I am trying to stay alive in my Martial Arts classes with Su Li. It's a close call at this moment. What can I do for you Jack?"

Jack asked to speak to Su Li.

Su Li came on the line and Jack could sense she was not winded or tired. "Yes Jack?" Jack asked her if Ethan was competent enough to skip the rest of her class today.

Su Li laughed, "Actually, he is doing quite well. I don't want him to get a "big head" so I push him harder when he excels. I don't think he'll fall too far behind by bowing out at this point."

Jack thanked her and asked to speak to Ethan again. When he came back on the line Jack told him, "Okay Ethan, I have arranged a life-saving end to your class today. Please get a shower and some street clothes and come to the living room in the next fifteen minutes to talk to me and Charlie."

Ethan agreed and hung up. He dried off his head and his hands and walked over to Su Li. "I'm sorry to break off our class today."

Su Li crunched up her eyebrows and asked, "Why are you sorry? Jack wants to talk to you and that takes precedence to the training."

Ethan smiled, "Yes Ma'am, I understand that; but, I am sad that it shortens my time with you."

Su Li's eyes widened as Ethan walked off for the showers.

CHAPTER TWENTY-SIX

Jack used his tablet so that he and Charlie could work up the transfer of authority from Charlie to Ethan as the manager of the COMSEC Department. Jack's prayers had assured him that Ethan would accept the position.

Jack sat back as they waited and asked Charlie, "Are you and Linda going to be okay simply being two of the Core Team and not being involved in everything that goes on with the team?"

Charlie nodded, "For a while we will still be involved with the higher functions of the COMSEC Department. I think Ethan will be a quick learner and we will be needed less and less for that role. I am going to suggest that we take over his new position as the prime investigators for team activities. That way I can still use the capabilities of the COMSEC group and also tap Ethan for ideas."

Jack realized that this whole switch could be a godsend for the team in several ways. He sensed the hand of God in this change; in fact, it seemed like a total God thing.

Ethan walked up and Jack asked him to sit down. Jack asked Ethan how his studies were going with everybody trying to cram everything from spy craft to Judeo-Christianity into his mind.

Ethan smiled, "I think I'm doing very well. In fact, Mark told me that I only needed to attend the refresher classes in combat and weapons training as I have reached a "satisfactory" rating in knowledge and tactics."

Charlie asked him how things were going with Ms. Li.

Ethan stopped for a second and then grinned. "Are you asking how "things" are going with Su Li, or are you asking how my classes in Martial Arts are going?"

Charlie grinned, "Yes."

Ethan looked a little pensive, but then grinned. "Things are going somewhere between very well to I just don't know yet."

Charlie said, "I see." A normally cryptic Asian response that didn't tell Ethan what he saw.

Jack sat back and asked Ethan, "Do you feel settled with being a part of the Crossfire Core Team?"

Ethan looked introspective for a few seconds and then answered, "Actually, I do feel comfortable as a part of the team and suddenly I have no idea what any other life the world could have to offer me. I doubt that playing first shooter video games would ever replace actually fighting demons."

Jack nodded, "I want to offer you a more difficult position with the team. I would like for you to replace Charlie and Linda Wu as the Director of COMSEC Services."

Ethan sat there and did not say anything for a few seconds as he tried to think out the change in his life this would bring. He looked up and said, "I think I would but I really have to pray about this before I say yes. Charlie alone would very hard to replace, as would Ms. Wu. Together, they will be a massive amount of talent and effort to replace that I doubt I am able to do alone."

Jack nodded, "Of course, but since time to accomplish this is extremely short may I suggest we three pray about it right now?"

Ethan had heard about the things that had been happening when Jack Malone prayed recently. But, Ethan thought, "In for a dime, In for a dollar". " Okay."

The three men joined hands in a small circle and Jack prayed for God's leading for the change in Ethan's position in God's Crossfire Team. He prayed seriously about the load and stress that would fall on Ethan and the great importance the position had for every team mission and operation. He also prayed for the Father's grace and mercy on Ethan so that he felt correctly positioned to handle the responsibility and command requirements necessitated by the position.

Ethan listened for God's direction with his heart more than his head. He had learned that the God of the Universe loved him more than he could imagine and was pleased at his efforts to walk a sinless and meaningful life before his Elohim. He relaxed as a power beyond his understanding bathed him in acceptance and power. This change was God's will for Ethan, he was never more sure of anything before in his life.

After the prayer, Ethan opened his eyes and knew that the answer he had received from God had also been communicated to Jack and Charlie.

Jack offered his tablet to Ethan for his signature sealing the deal. Ethan signed it and took a deep breath. "I know that Charlie is leaving really soon on the mission. How can I get the tools to do his job in such a short time?"

Charlie laughed, "We can do a transfer of command keys and passwords in just a few minutes. Plus, my associate, Crayton, can teach you everything that has been done and will remind you of everything that you must do.

Ethan sat there stunned, thinking to himself "Does he mean the Cray computer array would be my assistant or the other way around?"

Jack stood up and when Ethan also stood, Jack shook his hand. "I know you will do a great job and we expect you to have a learning curve as you assume control of the Department. I will go with you tomorrow and introduce you to the COMSEC employees as their new Director. This is a critical position in the Team and you will be compensated appropriately. Congratulations Ethan."

Ethan shook his hand and looked Jack square in the eyes. "You know that I will give a hundred and fifty per cent to the team."

CHAPTER TWENTY-SEVEN

With the COMSEC situation resolved, Jack went to one of the private rooms off of the living room and shut the door. He got on his knees and prayed for the Father to grant him the knowledge he needed to pray for the departing troops and to pray correctly for them while they were facing battle. He wanted to know how to pray effectively for these friends of his and warriors for God so that his prayer would have the correct impact on Heaven to give them God's backing, coverage of protection, and peace.

As he knelt there his heart was completely submitted to God in His Son's name to do what had been given to him to do. He had never done this before and he was going to do the Priest's duty properly to empower God to help them in their time of need. Jack felt tears falling from his eyes as he passionately plead with God to grant him the knowledge he needed for his people.

He sensed more than felt a change in his location. He opened his eyes and found he was kneeling in front of a chair. He stood up and turned around. Hugo sat in another chair several feet away. Jack sat down in the chair and said, "Hello Hugo, it is good to see you again."

Hugo smiled at Jack and nodded his head. "Hello Jack, yes it is good to meet you again. You have so completely given your life to the Most High that your prayers are exceptionally powerful. The prayer you were praying was exactly what you were asking for. Remember that the Most High is passionate like you are passionate. He desires His children to seek Him in humility and in passion for others. Do you know that none of what you were just praying was in any way for you? That is the type of prayer the Most High yearns for from his children. You were praying in Yahshua's Name and in Yahveh's Will for power to be used for God's Kingdom purposes. How can God not give you the desires of your heart in such a selfless plea? Do you understand?"

Jack thought about it and it made complete sense. "Hugo, I was only praying for God's protection and empowerment for the people that go into harm's way to do the work God has commanded. Is that my answer to how to pray for the team members going to battle and while they are in combat with the forces of darkness?"

Hugo nodded his head, "Yes, and like Solomon, you already tend to ask just for God's help for God's people without consideration for yourself other than the friendship you have with the people you're praying for in Yahshua's Name. Your reward will be great. Beware, lest the trappings of power and riches sway you to think more of yourself than you should. Be humble before your God. Pride is a basic access point of the evil one."

Jack nodded as he heard Hugo was warning him about ego and pride. These were things that had tripped him up before. Power and prestige and money did not sway him much but the warning was correct for him and he would heed it. "Hugo, when and how long should I pray for the warriors away in battle every day?"

Hugo smiled again. "When you feel the need to pray, or the urge to pray, is when you will pray for them. You need to realize that there is a connection in the spirit between the people you are anointed to be a Priest to and yourself. When they need prayer you will feel that need. At times you will rationalize a need to pray. Other times, God or the angels will tell you to pray for an individual or a cause. In other words, it will always be obvious when prayer is needed."

"Pray with honest, heart-felt passion and pour your heart out to the Lord for your people. You will know how long you need to pray each time, just follow the leading you get."

Jack realized he would learn to sense and respond to the demands of his new position. "Hugo, I appreciate your training and I want to be the best Priest I can be to these warriors. What else can you instruct me in concerning this position of Priest?"

Hugo taught Jack many things and what he should and should not do as a Priest of God to all people, but especially to the lambs given to him to lead as the Lord led him.

Jack found himself back in the meditation room full of energy and desire to fulfill his responsibilities as the Priest of the Crossfire Team. He got up and left the room for his apartment.

He found Laura sitting there cross-legged on her couch. She was obviously waiting for him.

Jack walked over and sat down in front of her. "I have some things to tell you I just heard from Hugo."

Laura smiled at him. "I know. In fact, I already know what you are going to tell me because Hugo just downloaded your meeting with him into my mind. He knows we need to speak the same words and do the same things in God's Name, so I got the home version of that same training."

Jack smiled back and took her hand. "I am so full of energy from that meeting. Is that how you are after your training sessions with Hugo?"

Laura nodded, "It is a total upper, that's for sure."

Jack called Mark and had him gather his team in the living room for prayer.

When everybody was present, Jack had them all kneel and he began to pray a heartfelt prayer for their victory, survival, and protection from anything the enemy could do to them. He placed his left hand on Mark's head and his right hand on Sarah's head. "Father Yahveh, in the glorious Name of your Son Yahshua I pray an anointing on Mark and Sarah Connelly that they can be a conduit for Your Word and Your Love to everyone they lead into battle. Fill them with Your power and Your Love Father, and keep them in the palm of Your hand constantly. Let Mark serve as their Priest in this matter and anoint him to truly speak Your words to them. Bring them all back to us, Father."

Jack then met with others of the SOG or the Core Team that wanted specific prayers and he prayed for them.

When he dismissed them he asked the Core Team members to remain behind. Jack followed God's leading to pray specifically for these three couples and two individuals to give them the strategic knowledge of Heaven to lead their forces and to win the battle." Then he and Laura blessed each one.

CHAPTER TWENTY-EIGHT

Mark woke up and took a quick shower and cleaned up for this fateful date. He thought, "I doubt that I will ever be able to use this on my resume but you have to admit that "Took War to the Gates of Hell" would be an interesting line item."

He gently shook the bed from the farthest corner from Sarah and said quietly, "Hey, Spy Lady, it's time to go kick demon butt for God."

Sarah yawned and stretched. She sat up in bed and smiled at Mark. "Oh, you are such a precautious man. Did you think I would wake up coming at you with weapons?"

Mark laughed, "Well, it's been known to happen before."

Sarah slid out from under the covers. "Well, this time I was awake before you were and was just lying there thinking about today. I came to realize I don't care if we live or die today but I desperately want to do my best for the Father and the team."

Mark keyed the Away Team all-call switch on his combat com set. "All Away Team members assemble at the Armory for launch inspection in thirty minutes."

Grabbing their gear, they walked down to the Armory and put their gear onto the floor. They waited quietly for the rest of the troops to show up. The other twenty-three warriors walked into the Armory and dropped their gear. They lined up in three lines and spaced themselves off from each other for inspection.

Mark took one line and Sarah took the other. Sarah took the third line while Mark went back to the front and said a few words to the troops. "Heads up people! I don't know just how long we've got before we appear in the demonic section we have been chosen to destroy. Make sure all of your ammo is the correct type and that you are locked and loaded because we could be dropped into a hot fire zone or very close to one. There may be no time for us to form up or even get set. If this is the case, pick your targets and shoot them. If there are any that don't die from the ammo, then revert to your prayers and armor and sword. Are there any questions?"

No hands were raised. "Okay, get your gear on and try to relax. I doubt it will be long before we are translated into our target zone. After we have accomplished our mission, I expect that we will be translated back here. If I'm wrong, then I don't recommend trying to walk out of Hell. We'll be given the help we need regardless of the situation."Mark called everyone to Attention. After they snapped to, he said, "Dismissed."

Everyone. including Mark and Sarah. strapped on, belted on or tied on all of their gear and then they waited.

There was a flash of white and Caleb appeared. "Everyone be ready. We will be there in three seconds. Three, two, one, now!"

In the next second the Armory disappeared and a Stygian darkness enveloped them. The darkness suddenly lightened and everything could be seen. There was a rancid, bitter dead meat aroma that was somewhere between horrible and really gross.

There were no demons around and the residents of this target seemed to be unaware of them so far. The other troops moved out toward their assigned areas to each floor of the domain, led by David and Alexis to the upper floor and Charlie and Linda toward the lower floor.

Mark led Sarah to the right which supposedly led to Moloch's throne room. So far the peace held with no combat. Mark pointed out the entrance to their target. He moved up next to the open doorway and quickly scanned the room. With hand signals he let Sarah know that there were ten to twenty demons in the room and that the one he figured was Moloch was seated above the others. Their plan was for Sarah to take on the regular demons while Mark dealt with the ancient evil itself.

Sarah held up three fingers, two fingers, and one finger. When the last finger dropped the two warriors slid into the room, moved apart and approached the raised area.

Everything was colored in the red spectrum, but visible. There were many indecipherable operations going on and little or no verbal communications. Both warriors could feel the urges to sin in all ways. Mark and Sarah were barely aware of the demonic pressures and sought all of their protection against the lures of the devil from God.

Sarah got the party going with a three-round burst that knocked over a large demon which then disappeared. She continued to shoot at the remaining demons as quickly as possible. Mark walked through the on-going slaughter, and focused all of his attention on the throne area. As he approached the gnarly old demon on the throne, the ancient creature hissed at Mark and made an obscene or obscure motion with one of its clawed hands. Mark dropped his right hand down and the spear with the Esteem of God flowing off of the tip appeared in his hand. He stepped up and hurled the spear at Moloch.

Two giant demons, and what Mark assumed was Satan, appeared. The two monstrous demons raised their rock solid shields and confidently stepped into the path of the spear to protect Moloch. The spear flashed through both of the shields and the demons. When the spear struck Moloch in the chest, the point of the spear exploded with the glory of God in such a brilliant flare that the walls and ceiling of that ancient room were brightly lit for the first time in known history. Satan recoiled from the Power of God and covered his eyes from the glare of Holy Light.

Mark had to admit that the scream or yell that the old demon-god Moloch made, as the fire on the spear tip shattered his body, was probably the most horrible sound he had ever heard.

As Moloch disappeared for the last time, Satan thundered his anger. "How dare you attack me and destroy my people? This is my world. By what authority do you battle here!"

Mark felt his voice taken over by Yahveh God, who spoke through him. *"Satan! You have defied me and dared me to stop you. I am stopping you and if you ever attempt to corrupt the human world like this again I will change prophesy and the rules and destroy you myself. Do you understand Me?"*

The hate and anger in Satan's eyes was a physical thing that was horrible to see. But, as Satan went down on one knee he locked eyes with Mark and said, "I hear and I obey Master." He then flashed out of sight.

By then Sarah had eliminated all of the other demons in the room. She came over to Mark and looked into his eyes. "Are you all right?" Mark tightened his lips in a straight line and said, "Yes, I think I'm all right.

He grabbed Sarah's arm and smiled at her. Then the two of them moved out to their secondary target areas.

Thousands of demons in the condemned section were attempting to flee the attacking warriors but the floor, walls, and ceilings were denied to them. God's white fire destroyed many of them when they attempted to flee through the structure. Many of the demons, realizing that there was no escape, turned to attack the warriors only to be destroyed by gunfire, explosions, or swords of the attackers. Hundreds of demons were destroyed by the rifle grenades because they were packed in so tightly that the flash of God's Esteem was conducted from one demon to another and they all disappeared.

As wave after wave of demons washed up against the team members they were sent to the pit at the hands of the attacking warriors. God's pure light flashed with every rifle shot, pistol shot, or grenade.

The demons that reached the warriors found them full of God's Holy Anger and vicious in battle. Denied their chance to attack the warriors or to escape the abattoir many demons turned on each other in frustration and took themselves and many other demons to the pit.

Mark and Sarah waded through the active demons and shot or blew up as many as possible. Demons could go through interior walls and seemed to came out of everywhere with black swords and clubs. Those that weren't killed that way were defenseless against the swords, shields, and the armor of the attackers.

Mark was astonished by the varieties in the types of demons in the place. Ugly wasn't even a category any longer, it was just normal. Mark got a call from David on the battle com that there was a new problem on the floor above them.

He signaled Sarah and they ran up the stairs to the problem floor and entered a huge room with very few demons in it. Ten of the team, led by David and Alexis, were shooting and battling the remaining demons in the room. The problem was two very large demons in the room and the ammunition with the Esteem of God wasn't stopping them. Two of the SOG and one of the Core Team were crumpled on the floor without their armor.

Mark grabbed a SOG warrior and inquired as to where these two came from. The man said, they just dropped in through the roof.

Mark looked at Sarah. "This wasn't in the plan. They can't get out, but they can get in. I think these are high level demons and there isn't enough God power in the bullets to stop them. Where are the missiles?"

Sarah used the COMM link to get two missiles to their location. Mark pointed out the two giant demons and the missile man lined up the first shot and fired. The shoulder-fired missile crossed the room in less than a second and impacted on the chest of the first demon. Mark could see the white light of God's power exploding through the demon and he could sense the demon successfully fighting the power. Mark told Sarah to get the second missile fired at the second demon.

As Mark ran across the room he saw that Alexis and David were in step with him. He prayed his battle hymn prayer with true passion. His armor and shield and sword appeared and the three of them added their sword's Esteem of God to the battle the first demon was trying to win. The additional attack drew the big demon's attention and it reached a huge hand down and swatted at Mark.

CHAPTER TWENTY-NINE

The giant hand of the demon must have weighted four hundred to five hundred pounds and it was swung with a tremendous aggravated anger. Mark knew that when the fist hit his armor he could expect to be smashed against the far wall and maybe die from the blow.

The distraction caused by the warrior's attack had allowed God's fire on the point of the missile to overcome the energy of the demon and the giant disappeared, suddenly. Mark was astonished when the giant fist disappeared without hitting him.

At that point Mark, David, and Alexis registered the explosion of the second missile on the second Arch-Angel level demon because the blast threw them all to the floor. The second demon apparently wasn't as good or powerful a fighter as the first one and it disappeared immediately.

Mark checked his body for damage and couldn't find anything important and the three warriors ran back to Sarah and looked around. There were no more demons to kill. He called out on the COMM set and found that the last demons had been destroyed and had disappeared. He had the team members search every inch of the floors to insure that really was the case.

Looking at Sarah he said, "Okay, primary mission is almost complete. Now, how should we destroy every atom in this area?"

Sarah had been praying and said, "Ask for Sergeant Holloway."

Mark called the Sergeant and had him report to their area. When the Sergeant reported, Mark asked him how to destroy the entire section of the demonic realm that they were in, down to the last atom.

The Sergeant pulled a spare backpack off his shoulder and took out a heavy plastic bag. He handed it to Mark. Mark opened the bag and took out the device inside. One look and he knew what they needed to do. "Okay, get all the troops up here, Now!

When the entire twenty-seven warriors that made up the Away team assembled in the room of the giant demons, Mark said, "Ladies and Gentlemen, I want to congratulate you on your victory in God's name."He held up the device. "What you are looking at is a 500 Kiloton tactical nuclear weapon. I am going to set this bomb off to accomplish God's command of destroying this place down to the last atom."

"Let's try to stay together as a group in case the Father wants to use a single bus to take us all home in."

Mark prayed that God would protect them from the nuclear blast and anything else they'd run into after they disintegrated the section they were in. He got a word from Yahveh God that Satan was marshaling his forces to destroy the team completely and rebuild the effort to destroy the world with a new fire god. The word from Heaven implied that Satan would need the processes in the existing area to accomplish their continuation of the project. They only had seconds before they were overwhelmed.

Mark set the bomb down on a structure that might have been a table. He looked at his wife and said in a loud voice, "God says that Satan is about to overwhelm us and regain this area and this despicable effort. We cannot allow that to happen." It was obvious to all the team members that they would have to make the ultimate sacrifice to complete God's work here. Mark could see the agreement in everyone's eyes. He took Sarah's hand and he flipped the switch on the nuclear bomb.

Expecting instant disintegration Mark staggered as he suddenly found himself and Sarah in the Armory again. He looked up and counted noses. He told Sarah later that he could have counted feet but then he would have to divide by two to get the real number, noses were easier. Everyone was there including the damaged and the dead.

Mark walked over to the unmoving bodies and saw that two of the SOG troops had died from sword wounds from the enemy puncturing their armor somehow. He turned over the last body and realized it was Sean Murphy.

The surviving troops had more or less collapsed on the floor or benches from the release of the stress of what they had just done and the amazing fact that they weren't dead.

Jack, Laura, Su Li and Ethan Reaper ran into the Armory and congratulated the troops. Jack and Laura walked over to the three bodies on the floor and Laura gasped when she saw Sean. Looking at the three dead team members she covered her mouth with her hand and tears came.

One of the weary warriors dropped to her knees next to Sean's body and put her hand on his chest. Jack saw that it was Megan Cole. She prayed a quick prayer for Sean and got up to go. Laura pulled the young woman to her and held her as they both broke down in tears.

Sergeant Holloway came over to the group by Sean. "I saw what happened to him. One of the SOG women had been beaten so hard by the demons that she passed out and her armor disappeared. She was instantly killed by a demonic sword.

Sean cut the head off of the demon. He then tried to help the woman on the floor. You must realize that there were dozens of demons attacking us at that point and one got through and ran a thin black blade through Sean's back and out his front. He collapsed so fast it must have gone through his heart.

Charlie and Linda Wu had limped over to the growing group and confirmed the Sergeant's testimony. Linda said, "It was beyond Sean's nature to leave a comrade wounded on the ground in the middle of an attack without seeing if there was anything that could be done to save them."

Charlie frowned, "I thought the armor could deflect anything like that. It didn't seem to affect the blade at all. I killed the demon that struck Sean but the knife disappeared with the demon.

Jack prayed for the pain and loss that each one of the friends and, especially, the families of all three the dead warriors. Then he had two of the non-Away team SOG members get the three bodies into body bags and take them to the Mossad side of the base for an Autopsy.

Jack got the surviving members together and prayed for them and that the Father would revive their spirits after the battle and cover their wounds for the lost. He congratulated them for a job well done. Jack looked up and said, "I had a visit from Caleb before I came down here and he reported that the nuclear bomb you guys used eliminated all record of Moloch's efforts and that operation will not be repeated." That resulted in a loud cheer from everybody there.

Mark had everybody turn in their gear, do their after-action reports and then head to their rooms and showers.

Jack put his hand out and stopped Mark and Sarah from leaving. He looked at Mark. "Caleb said that we need to pray for you, immediately."

The four of them walked over to a small conference room near the Armory and Jack had both Mark and Sarah sit down. Laura stood behind Sarah and put her hands on Sarah's shoulders while Jack did the same for Mark.

Jack started praying, "Most Heavenly Father Yahveh, I come before you today seeking your Holy Spirit to cleanse Mark and Sarah from the effects of the evil one."

Jack felt the heaviness and prayed into it. "Holy Spirit of God you know the seeds of death that Satan planted in your children Mark and Sarah. I plead with you now that you wash them in the Blood of the Lamb from the Seven Places He shed His Blood. Completely root out anything demonic or sinful, planted by Satan in these two warriors, break off any curses they impressed on them and any they will ever try to place on them. Remove any assignments and any strongholds and let the Light of Yahshua fill them from the soles of their feet to the top of their heads, from fingertip to fingertip and in all eleven dimensions. It is in Yahshua's most Holy Name we pray."

Mark looked up. "That old snake did curse me while bowing his knee to Yahshua who was speaking through me."

Jack nodded, "It is his nature to condemn everybody and everything constantly and he managed to do the same to Sarah."

Laura was about to speak when the angel Caleb appeared in the room with them. He reached over and placed his fingers over Mark's eyes for a second. The he released Mark and looked at Jack. "The devil is in the details. Not only did he curse Mark but he did it through his eyes. God wanted me to ensure that nothing Satan did in the few seconds he was face to face with Mark would remain or fester. Mark is now completely clear of the curses, effects, and future effects of that contact. I am honored to be known to this man that stood up to Satan himself."

Caleb repeated his efforts with Sarah and disappeared. Jack pulled Mark up from his seat and hugged him. "I am so glad you two are still with us. We love you both and really need you."

Sarah smiled as she got up. She hugged both Jack and Laura and put her arm around Mark. "We really appreciate your love and prayers for us." She looked at Mark while speaking to Jack. "I don't know if Mark was aware of it because he had just destroyed Moloch and was in a staring contest with Satan at the time, but I distinctly felt your prayers for us. Wow! That was so important and uplifting. To just know you were praying for us at that time."

Jack laughed, "I wasn't the only one praying for you guys you know. Everyone else on the team and my dad, mom, and uncle were on our knees praying our hearts out for you."

Mark asked, "Where was the Sensei?"

Jack grinned, "He's somewhere in either Tel Aviv or Jerusalem studying the Israeli Krav Maga Martial Arts.

CHAPTER THIRTY

Jack convened the After-Action Review and Summary (AARS) on the trip to Hell the next afternoon.

Ethan had worked with Crayton and had picked out the highlights and worked them into several montages. He had one each for all the Core Team leaders, and a memorial montage for Sean Murphy.

They reviewed all the Montages and the Summaries, including the one from Sean's camera and his voice notes. He was doing just as the witnesses agreed. He had tried to save the woman on the floor when he was attacked and killed from behind while he knelt over Captain Carol Norwood. Megan said in a quiet voice. "He died doing what he liked best. He will be missed."

Jack said, "You'll see him again, soon."

Megan looked introspective for a few seconds and then smiled, "That's right isn't it? But I will still miss him until then."

Jack returned to Mark's camera record and the inserted image of Satan dropping to one knee and glaring daggers at Mark. Jack shook his head, "He doesn't look happy. I think we really ticked off the ultimate evil on the planet. But, I have to admit that Ethan did a great job of reproducing Moloch and Satan from your After-Action reports."

Mark smiled faintly, "That is what the Father wanted us to do, to send Satan a message. I think we accomplished our mission to a tee. I just hope that Ole Beelzebub was far enough away from our final gift that we didn't singe his tail scales."

A strong, calm voice that was somewhat familiar from the back of the room said, "He was far enough away but he sacrificed over six thousand demons in the blast. He believed that you all died in that explosion. Unfortunately, he found out later that wasn't true."

Jack looked at the back of the room and saw the Archangel Raquel in his jeans and pull-over shirt.

Jack smiled, "Hello Raquel. Introduce yourself to the people here that did not have a chance to meet you last time."

Raquel stood up and walked to the front of the group. He turned around and smiled. "Hello, my name is Raquel and I work for the same God you work for. I'm a general contractor with special skills that are used wherever necessary. I hope to have a chance to work with all of you this time because I may be here indefinitely on this latest assignment." He turned to Jack. "As everyone here and back at the office expected, you have refocused Satan's ire and attention from the many major plans he had to only one. You can guess what that is. I'm here to prevent inappropriate responses on his part."

Mark stood up and walked up to Raquel and shook his hand. "Welcome aboard Raquel, I am really glad you are here. We may have stirred up a hornet's nest but I for one think we can encourage the adversary to look to other places for satisfaction, don't you?"

Raquel sighed, "Mark, you live up to your reputation. I can honestly say that I have not met any man or angel that has the unmitigated gall to kick Satan in the backside and then offer to do it some more so he will look other places for revenge. It will be an honor and a privilege to work with you on this assignment."

Jack asked Raquel, "Are there any precautions we should be taking right now?"

Raquel looked thoughtful for a bit, and then shook his head. "Satan is aware that I am here now so he will not do anything without a solid plan. Of course, you just delivered him a major slap from God on his illegal operations. You have to understand that this successful raid in his own realm has made him look foolish to all the powers that be. So, even though he has to ask permission to attack you, he will. And he knows that Carol will see any of his permitted actions. That is a bit of a restraint on his revenge. I think he will carefully craft his response to the Crossfire Team and we will need to be on guard for just about <u>anything</u>."

Raquel's stress on the last word was a wake-up call that they were dealing with Satan himself and that was to be treated with caution and understanding of the power involved.

Mark asked, "Raquel, how is the Queen-to-be in England doing since our trip there?"

Raquel looked at Mark for a minute. The he said, "Abigale Berton-Smythe is more than holding her own with the enemy. She is now walking so close to Yahshua she is filled up with the Light of His righteousness that the enemy cannot even get close to her. As they try then we are there to remind them not to do that."

CHAPTER THIRTY-ONE

As the team meeting ended, David Zahavy came up to Mark and Jack and asked if they could talk for a few minutes. The two men looked at each other and nodded.

They let the others go on to their duties or whatever they needed to do and sat down with David. Raquel sat down with them. David grinned, "I don't think I've ever had a conference at this high of a level before."

Jack asked what David had for them. David nodded, "Remember when we brought Eli Moreh to the Sea Base?" Everyone nodded including the angel. "I checked in to the situation of Eli's sister, who couldn't get help from the Jewish community because she is a Messianic Jew. It seems that her husband divorced her after they had three children and still isn't pleased with her for not doing things his way. He is a Tel Aviv native and is a third level manager in the Tel Aviv-Yafo Municipality."

"He has used his office and his position to punish Eli's sister, his ex-wife. He has black-balled her from getting any public service help or even any emergency help if she or the kids have a medical problem. He has made sure that she cannot get a job if there is any connection to his part of the government and is apparently keeping tabs on her by city surveillance and police reports. His name is Shimon Ketzlya. Eli's sister has gone back to her maiden name of Tamar Moreh."

"I also have several unsubstantiated reports that Ketzlya has personally harassed her neighbors and threatened them if they do anything to help her or assist her. This flies directly against God's laws for Hebrews. Torah says that they are required to help widows and orphans. They are also supposed to help the needy. This is charity, which in Israel is called Tzedakah. Apparently this man is so embittered by losing his family he is willing to do anything to make her life a living Hell on earth in revenge even though he drove them away."

David looked at the two men he admired greatly. "Is there anything we can do about this?"

Jack sat back in his chair and thought about the situation. Mark waited quietly for Jack's decision. Jack sat up again. "In this particular situation we can do lots of things to help the sister of one of our employees. We hired Eli three days ago. What did you have in mind, David?"

"Well, I have already paid to have her relocated to a much better neighborhood and gave her a new name for the time being so that Shimon Ketzlya can't find her through his business or police contacts. She has been able to put her kids into a private Messianic School that is discrete. I've arranged things so that she has adequate food and supplies and a car. I convinced her to change her looks so that Mr. Ketzlya can't use the police facial recognition to re-locate her. I've gotten her a cell phone that is in no way connected to her old life or his life at all. I took Eli there and explained what is going on and he has been very grateful because he won't get his first paycheck from us for several weeks. I gave him an advance that should tide him over."

Jack nodded, "All good stop-gap measures. I take it, knowing you, that you're using your own money to do these things, right?"

David smiled, "Of course I am."

Jack jotted a note down on his tablet. "Okay, I've just created an account for the team that you can use to replace your funds and draw on as needed in the future."

David raised his hands palm outward to stop Jack. "I thank you for that and it may come in handy in the future. But, we live in Israel and now that all of you have taken Israeli citizenship you need to learn about how things are done by your neighbors here."

"I have far more money than I can probably ever spend. Plus, Alexis is totally on board on this and she also has more money than she needs. In Israel it is an honor and a Torah Commandment to help the less fortunate than you. There is an axiom from Bible scripture that says "To get a blessing from God, you first must be a blessing to others. I am glad to spend my money to help these people. It is my way of acquiring God's blessings in my life. Jack, you don't want to block my or Alexis' blessings now, would you?"

Jack grinned and shook his head. "No, David, I would not want to block your blessings. But, I think we need to resolve Tamar's situation before her ex-husband finds her again and we need to do it in a way that will prevent this man from ever misusing his power and doing this again to anybody. Any ideas?"

Raquel tapped the table and got everyone's attention. Jack nodded at the angel.

Raquel spoke clearly and quietly. "The way the Most High would resolve this would be to reverse the man's situation so that he learns what life is like being harassed by someone like himself. Then he could make the choice to mend his ways or not. If he mends his ways, he could gradually be restored to his previous level of power and authority with a much higher view of life. If he decides in his bitterness or anger to not to bow his knee to God, then he would remain in his sin."

Jack nodded, "I agree, but how do we arrange that here on Earth?"

Raquel smiled, "You forget, I am in both places, on Earth and in Heaven. Would you like me to arrange those things to happen to Shimon Ketzlya? He is not a Jewish believer by the way."

Jack looked at David who sat there stunned by the possibilities. David thought it out and shook his head. "No, Raquel, we must not attempt to play God in these people's lives. It is wrong in Torah and it would be witchcraft and open a door for the devil who would dearly love that right now."

Raquel nodded his head. "That is Torah, David Zahavy. I was interested in how you would decide that issue. You are quite passionate in your desire to change her circumstances but you are wise enough not to "play God" as you say."

Raquel thought for several minutes and just as Jack was about to say something the angel spoke. "Since you were wise enough not to exceed your position even though you could have attempted it through me, I can tell you that part of the problem is already being resolved through the man's own actions. There is no action needed in Heaven to change his circumstances. His misuse of his authority has already led him down a dark path and the results of that misuse are becoming apparent in his life right now. Some of Tamar's neighbors have gotten a lawyer and are threatening to sue his Municipality for allowing him to try to influence them incorrectly. His job has been taken away from him and he is facing several misdemeanor charges and a felony charge related to his strong-arm tactics, according to the District Attorney. This will all happen by next week in your time. As long as Tamar Moreh doesn't try to save him from himself he will learn his lessons and could be able to make the right decisions."

David nodded his head. "I will make sure she doesn't hear about his predicament so she won't try to save him. I think that is all right and that I'm not trying to manipulate her future.

David rethought that concept. "Oh no! I AM trying to manipulate her future and that is witchcraft. Father, forgive me for trying to do your job for you."

Raquel looked at something distant and then nodded, "David, you have been forgiven. But you must remember what you just learned. Humans seem to rush to judgment and try to pull strings to have things come out the way they want them to rather than praying and trusting in the Most High."

CHAPTER THIRTY-TWO

Jack looked at David. "It seems that Heaven has your charity case well in hand. Why don't you get Ethan to let you take Eli over to Tamar's place and talk to the two of them. If I understand you correctly, David, the funds you've used for Tamar and her children, are a gift or a blessing. Explain that to them if they don't understand it. I think Eli is beginning to see the Father through you and it can only get better for him after that."

David agreed and Jack prayed for him, Eli, Tamar, the children, and for Shimon, that they would all learn the truth of God's Son and the Torah. Jack suddenly captured a thought that had been nagging him since the Road to Hell battle. He called Ethan and requested him, and Crayton of course, to review the three people killed on that trip and see if they could figure out how the enemy swords or knives were able to penetrate the armor that God had given them. Ethan agreed and hung up.

David left and Raquel explained that he had to "do" some things and he would be back soon. He vanished and Jack and Mark were alone for a while. Jack looked at Mark. "Well, did all that go all right?"

Mark nodded, "I think it did and I don't know about you but I learned two lessons since I walked in here. One is about Jewish Tzedakah and the other is about Torah and not playing God. That's about all I can absorb today. I'm going home and rest."

Jack agreed with his friend. "Me too, everything has been pretty well wrapped up here anyway."

Mark slapped Jack on the back and said as he parted ways with his friend, "Well, in the end this day was just another walk in the park."

Jack walked into his apartment to find himself alone. He remembered forgetting to check on Laura several battles back when she had been captured and he wasn't even aware of it for almost a half of a day. He quickly keyed his microphone and, with some urgency, asked for her to respond.

Laura came back immediately. "Yes, Jack?"

Jack sighed in relief. "Are you all right?"

Laura confirmed her safety. "I'm in the SOG area and talking with Megan Cole. I think she had feelings for Sean and it is taking a little time to get over the emotions of the loss. I'm sorry; I should have told you where I was."

Jack said, "That's all right, I could have just looked at the locator screen and seen where you were. I'm just glad that you are all right."

Laura was slightly miffed by his assumption that she was an easy mark for enemy action but that was offset by the warm feeling she had that he worried about her enough to make sure she was all right. "I like the fact that you take care of me."

Jack said, "Oh, guess what. We've got an old friend as a visitor for a while."

Laura thought over all their old friends but didn't make a connection to what Jack was talking about. "Who is our old friend that we haven't seen for a while?"

Jack laughed, "It's Raquel, the Archangel we went to Britain with a while ago. He's here to help keep Satan from doing anything too evil to us."

Laura was pleased to hear that the Father was protecting them in the person of Raquel. "Say "hi" for me, I may be here for a few more hours."

Jack hung up and looked at his bed. He thought to himself, "Maybe I am tired after all. I think I'll take a short nap."

Just to make sure he wasn't deluding himself he prayed to see if a nap was in God's Will for him. Apparently it was as he didn't get a negative response. So he dimmed the lights and turned down the air conditioning so that it was not only dark but also cool. He lay down and was sound asleep in minutes. In the spiritual dimension Rose asked Caleb, "I'm worried about all the team members this time. Satan is furious about these Godly people and will do anything he can to destroy them. Can we keep them from harm?"

Caleb made a noncommittal shrug of his shoulders. "If it comes our way, we will make a stand. Beyond that it is up to the Most High to keep them safe."

CHAPTER THIRTY-THREE

Life went back to a normal schedule for most of the people in the Crossfire Team in the Undersea Base off of the Israeli coast. The action board was curiously empty and there were no calls from the Mossad or the Kidon.

Jack prayed that the Father would enlighten him as to the cause of this unusual quietness. He figured that Satan was holding back on his illegal activities, temporarily of course. The time granted to them was used to clean everything, update anything that was worn, improve and replace anything with a better version, and a major focus on continual training and exercise. Jack cleared out his complete backlog of paperwork and projects. Even his "Honey Do" list was empty for the first time since his marriage to Laura.

Jack called the Israeli tax attorney he had hired to make sure that the team met their obligation to Israel in that area. The principal taxes in Israel that would affect them were income tax and a capital gains tax. The VAT (Value Added Tax) and land appreciation taxes did not affect them. The primary law on income taxes in Israel is codified in the Income Tax Ordinance. Offsetting their income and capital gains taxes were special tax incentives for new immigrants to encourage *Aliyah* or the return to Israel incentives.

Joseph Bloomberg had taken on the account for the Crossfire Team in good faith seeing a profitable client with people that had become citizens recently. He wasn't aware of their special ranking and position within the Jewish community and the government until he had special visitors from the Prime Minister's office, the Mossad, and a personal visit from one of the most important people in Israel, Rabbi Simon ben Chanan.

Joe's understanding of what the Crossfire Team did for a living had taken on a whole new importance after his meetings with these various organizations. This importance took on a unique imperative that he fully understood after seeing the video the Mossad showed him of a street battle with the Goyim where the Crossfire Team was defending the city and the public. He had been warned to take extremely good care of this account and made aware of multiple incentives not available to people who were not working directly with God on a daily basis.

Joe listened to Jack Malone as he amended the information that had been submitted to Joe's company due to additional operations (Mr. Malone called them missions) that had occurred recently. Joe thanked Mr. Malone for the information and hung up. He had only suggested they meet at Mr. Malone's business one time. That wasn't going to happen. Joe amended the paperwork and filed it away carefully. He was fairly sure that there was probably a Mossad accountant somewhere that was duplicating his work and he wanted to remain squeaky clean on everything he did on this account. Joe didn't advertise he had this account either. He had been warned about the aggressiveness of some of the competition that the Crossfire Team had to work against. He understood the unspoken indications to consider the competition as enemies.

During the lull Captain Eckhart of the SOG got bad news. His father had passed away due to a heart attack. The funeral would be tomorrow in Omaha, Nebraska at five in the afternoon.

He told his four friends about the trip he had to make to Omaha to speak at his father's funeral. The two men and two women offered to support him and go with him to the funeral.

The Captain requested a two-day leave for himself and the other four members. Leave was granted for all five members with the condolences of the rest of the Crossfire Team at the loss of his father. Due to the time constraints the Captain had arranged for a private jet to take them to Omaha and back.

After leaving Ben Gurion Airport in Tel Aviv, Israel the $11.5 million dollar Learjet 70 banked left toward Netanya and the Mediterranean Sea. The plane suddenly pitched forward and dived into the ground at 300 miles per hour, instantly killing everyone on board.

The Israeli Police and the IDF Military ruled out any terrorist involvement and left it to the CAA to determine the cause of the accident. Ethan Reaper had eased into all of the Police, IDF, and CAA files to investigate the accident. He read the secret CAA report of the accident after the cockpit data recorders which are called "Black Boxes", had been found and read. He copied the report and eased out of the CAA computer system. He took the copy to the War Room and found Jack and Laura there. He asked them if they could have Su Li join them.

Laura smiled, "Missing your teacher?"

Ethan smiled back. "Yeah, actually I do, quite a bit, but this is business."

Su Li jogged over to the War Room and sat down in her seat. Ethan put the file up on the big screen. "I'm sure we have a murder case here instead of an accident investigation. The CAA interrogated the Black Boxes from the Lear Jet that crashed and five of the SOG team were lost. I've highlighted the important things." He showed the text portion and played an audio clip from the aircraft just before it nosed over and crashed. Everyone heard a nasty grating voice that was as cold as the grave. "Let me do the flying you insignificant insect. This was followed by a short male scream and the words, "No, no, no!" A third voice was heard saying "Get away from the controls, demon." There was an extremely evil laugh and then the sounds of the crash and the end of the recording.

Ethan said, "I found out that the scream and the second voice was that of the civilian pilot and the last voice was that of Captain Eckhart. The first voice and the laugh were noted as unrecognized."

Jack was angry enough to break things in the vicinity of his workstation. He looked up and yelled, "Raquel!"

Raquel appeared next to Jack, "Yes, Jack?"

Jack swung around in his chair and stared at the Arch Angel. "Satan just had five of our people killed in retaliation for our raid on Hell. Weren't you here to help us stop anything like this?"

Raquel didn't react to the anger in Jack's voice but instead asked, "Did Miss Moffet have any inclination of this attack from the matrix?"

Jack called Carol and asked her about the aircraft accident.

Carol replied, "Nothing, Jack. There hasn't been anything related to aircraft or an attack on the team for four days. That was so weird I checked with Hugo and he confirmed my readings. Why?"

Jack had calmed down slightly, "Because Satan just killed five of our SOG troops on the way to one of their father's funeral."

Carol was obviously sad and irritated herself. "Then he did it illegally. I don't have any demon authorized to do anything like attack our team members or an aircraft. Jack thanked her and hung up. He looked at Raquel and said, "She and Hugo said that there was no plan approved by God for Satan to kill them."

Raquel thought for a few seconds. "Stay here!" The thought that went through Jack's mind was; "Where would we go?"

Raquel reappeared and stared at the three team members. "I reported to the Most High that Satan has again caused human deaths and that of Crossfire Team members no less, without Heaven's approval. The Most High looked at the event Himself and determined that Satan had orchestrated the entire operation. In other words, Satan, again, knowingly defied a direct commandment of God so that he could accomplish revenge on the people who destroyed Moloch and the fire god's domain.

Yahveh God implicitly told Satan that He would not allow Satan to continue this type of defiance. Therefore, the Most High has restored all that was destroyed and has summoned Satan to account for his actions."

Jack looked at the Arch Angel. "By "restored all that was destroyed", does that mean he restored the SOG forces to life?"

Raquel nodded his head, "And, Captain Eckhart's father and the pilot of the aircraft and the aircraft. Except for the people in this group the memories of everything that has happened has been expunged."

Su Li asked, "I can understand the pilot, the passengers, and the aircraft being restored but why was Captain Eckhart's father restored from his heart attack?"

Raquel looked at Su Li. "Because the demon was the cause of Mr. Eckhart's heart attack. It should not have happened at this time."

Jack put a call into the SOG and asked to speak to Captain Eckhart. When the SOG soldier came on the line, Jack arranged for a meeting with him later that afternoon.

Jack hung up and turned to Raquel, "Will my discussing this with him cause any problems?"

Raquel shook his head. "He won't remember any of the entire sequence of events but it could serve as a warning to the personnel of the SOG of the battles to come."

CHAPTER THIRTY-FOUR

Laura sat at her workstation in the War Room and looked at Jack. "I was happy to hear that your parents and your Uncle Larry are keeping busy at the Messianic Synagogue, but aren't they at risk being outside the Sea Base?"

Jack nodded, "Raquel says that there are angels assigned to each one of them and to the members we left in the states. They will call on Caleb and Rose, along with Raquel, if needed."

Jack looked a little irritated. "Raquel told me that God is most pleased to help us because we raided Moloch's little garden of delights. It seems that less than one in fifty million people would have done that."

Laura stared at him. "What's the matter, sweetheart? Are you upset that you didn't have the opportunity to go to Hell with Mark?"

Jack looked confused for a few seconds and then made the connections to what Laura was saying. "No, no, I'm upset that fifty million people would not do that for God if he asked. I don't think that we missed anything by not going on the "Road Trip to Hell" with Mark. Look what God in Heaven has assigned for us to do as the Priest and Priestess of this demon butt-kicking group. Wow!! Our prayer life is going right out of this world, literally. I see our close connection to Yahveh as bringing us to the highest level we have ever seen."

Laura smiled at her husband. His enthusiasm was contagious and she had felt the same things as Jack. She sighed when it dawned on her that she had asked God to give them more of a family life than just running and shooting and sword fighting all the time. She thought, "Well, I asked for it, so I guess this is the response to that prayer."

There was a knock on the doorframe to the War Room. Jack looked up and saw Captain Eckhart standing there. Jack motioned for him to come into the room.

Jack shook his hand and had him sit down. He liked the Captain and was very glad that God in His Mercy had reinstated the five members of the SOG to life. He looked at the Captain and said. "You have no idea about any of this but I want to tell you that you're the best looking corpse I've ever seen."

The Captain tipped his head to the side and looked strangely at Jack. "General, I don't understand that comment."

Jack smiled broadly. "Let me tell you a story about you and four of your best friends and your father. Two days ago you had been informed by your mother that your father had passed away from a heart attack. You were asked to speak at the Eulogy. Your four friends decided to support you and go to Omaha with you. You rented a Lear Jet 70 for the trip as it was too late to get commercial tickets in time to be there. Twelve miles out of Ben Gurion Airport the plane nosed over and crashed into the earth at three hundred miles per hour. The pilot, you, and all four of your friends died instantly."

The Captain was still unsure that Jack had not lost his senses. Jack touched a control on his panel. "This recording does not exist anywhere in the world today, except here. He let the video run as the announcer stood before the still smoldering ruins of the Lear Jet telling the world that Captain Eckhart and two women and two men plus the pilot had been killed in the crash. Their pictures were shown at the bottom of the picture.

Jack turned off the video and shook his head. "We had lost all of you to a revenge action on Satan's part." Jack played the Black Box audio tape and the Captain heard his own voice on the recording. He looked at Jack, "Then why am I still here listening to this?"

Raquel suddenly appeared in his angelic persona."Because it wasn't your time to die. Satan improperly arranged for you and the others, including your father, to die. God restored everything so that righteousness would be fulfilled. This, that Satan meant for evil, God has turned into good. Use this warning to educate the other people in the team about being wary in all things. If something doesn't seem right, bring it to Jack or Laura."

Raquel vanished. Jack sighed. "He's right Captain. We need to remain on guard until our time on Earth is completed."

Captain Eckhart sat back and smiled. "Thank you for telling me about this miracle. My faith is even more uplifted to know that God would do that for me. I think I'll wait until I get the men and two women that died with me alone before I tell them about our second return from an encounter with Satan and his imps."

CHAPTER THIRTY-FIVE

After the Captain had left, Jack got up and felt unsettled in his Spirit. He told Laura he was going to pray. She had received a phone call and nodded her head at his announcement.

Jack wanted to isolate himself so he went to the apartment and got on the bed and set the controls so that he was floating on the sea with nothing around him. He lay down, closed his eyes, and listened to the waves on the beach below him.

He started to praise the Father in Heaven and felt his Spirit rise to meet the Most High in true worship. He suddenly felt released from his uneasiness. The freedom was phenomenal and it filled him with hope and purpose. He saw his team on one side of a transparent wall and the darkness that was the world of Satan and the demons on the other side of the wall.

The darkness was constantly mixing and roiling around seeking any way through or around the wall. On his side there was peace and contentment mixed with wariness about the darkness. He saw the darkness as a threat to his team and he petitioned God to protect them and end the constant threat by the darkness.

God spoke and the team started to disassemble a part of the wall and Jack worried that the enemy would flood through the hole, but it didn't. Jack saw himself and Mark leading the team to connect a square pipe to the wall at the hole. He watched as he turned a large handle and the brilliant white contents of the pipe began to flow into the darkness and overcome it. Soon there was just a small part of the dark side of the wall that held any darkness and that was surrounded by white light in all directions and Jack felt that the darkness was surrendering to the light.

Jack came awake and sat up on the bed. He played the dream over in his mind. He bowed his head and asked God for an interpretation to the dream. While he was waiting he did lie down on the bed again and soon fell asleep. He woke up several hours later and saw that it was already

6:00P.M. He recalled the dream and the fact that he hadn't gotten an answer to what it meant. He knew then that God wanted him to think it out.

He assumed that the wall separating the light and the darkness was the inter-dimensional wall between the normal human dimension and the spiritual dimension of the demons. He assumed that since the enemy couldn't get through or around the wall that God had decreed the barrier solid against the darkness, at least for a time.

Their praying and God responding was straight forward. But, what did God tell them and what was meant by the team making a hole in the dimensional wall? What was the square hose and what was filling it? What handle did he turn to let the white power into the dark area and fill it up?

The white power filling the hose was probably the Esteem or Glory of God like that on the swords. So it was something that connected to the Glory of God that would be let loose in the dark dimension and fill it up. The hole in the dimensional wall was something that the team would create. Why wouldn't the enemy flow through the hole? He needed more brain power than he had by himself. He prayed that the Father would let him converse with Raquel about this dream.

Jack noticed that Raquel was standing next to the bed. Jack described the dream and what he had deduced so far.

Jack asked Raquel, "Do you understand this dream that I believe that Yahveh gave to me?"

Raquel said, "I do understand the symbols represented in the dream. The wall you describe is the inter-dimension wall between your dimension and that of the demons as you assumed. The hole in the wall will be another incursion into the demonic domain by this team. The hose or pipe will be the power of Yahveh and the presence of Yahshua directed against Satan and his demons. In your vision, when you signal the attack, it's presented as you turning the lever or valve. After you have introduced or inserted the perfect Will of God to that demonic realm, there is only a remnant of evil left."

"The remnant is the obedient power of evil that will not break Yahveh's covenant. This will sap Satan's strength in his quest to destroy your team. But, this is years in the doing until the resolution. This is Yahveh's sign to you that the eternal battle will eventually be won and you and the team will be reason it will be so."

Jack sighed, "Thank you, Raquel. Will you be with us until the "resolution"?"

Raquel smiled, "Perhaps, but, I will only be here as you need my efforts because Heaven has other tasks for me to accomplish during the same period."

The angel's eyes seemed to glow with golden fire as he looked at Jack. "Do not be discouraged or fearful. As the Priest of this team your strength and determination must be a steadfast pillar of power and strength. They will need you and Laura to lead and guide them as the world grows darker under the rule of the Anti-Christ and the False Prophet."

"Do you not understand that the two of you have been chosen and are being refined to share the love and strength of determination of Yahveh to your team as you become the man and woman that Yahveh desires? You two need to be an inspiration to the men and women of the team in the days to come. You and Laura together are also going to fulfill the roles of Prophet and Healer as well as leaders and Priests. There will be times this war will take all the strength and will you and Laura have together to forge onward for the team against the power of evil in the Universe. Rose, Caleb, as well as I and many of the angelic host will stand with you. While in Earth's time it is only about three years until God calls you home; the number of missions the Crossfire Team will face is considerably greater than you would expect."

Jack looked at the long war ahead of the team and realized that this is where the God of the Universe had been leading them since the inception of the group in Denver four years ago. They had been led and nurtured on their path to mature them as a team that would stand as a force for Yahveh during this time. His prayer was for the strength of God to enable him, his wife, and everyone on the whole team to stand for God and His Kingdom. And, when they had finished the battle, to continue and still stand.

Jack said in a quiet voice to the angel. "I need my wife to hear what we've just discussed so that she understands the full commitment required."

Laura walked over and sat on the end of the bed. "I came in at the same time Raquel appeared. He had me stay in the background while you sought the truth and worked out the understanding of the dream and our future with him."

Jack looked at the woman he loved more than his own life and said, "I have committed you as well as myself to this course that Yahveh has laid out before us. I know that your greatest desire is to please the Father. Now you can see the rough road to accomplish that in front of us. Laura, I desperately need you to walk this road with me or I will fail."

She smiled and put her hand on Jack's. "I want to walk every mile of this road with you and would do it with no other man."

Raquel said, "So be it in the name of the Most High Elohim." And he faded from sight leaving the two people to contemplate their future.

CHAPTER THIRTY-SIX

Jack and Laura walked down the stairs from the apartment level to go to the War Room when they found themselves in a beautiful, cloud-like room with angelic singing filling the air around them. Jack looked at Laura with a raised eyebrow as if to say, "What now?"

Jack quickly recognized that the righteousness and purity that flowed over them was an elemental part of the person of Yahshua. He fell to his knees along with Laura and saw a great assemblage of witnesses around them. He recognized Raquel, Hugo, Caleb, and Rose who were singing a mighty song of praise along with many other angels.

The Son of God walked out of what Jack thought of as a sunburst of golden beams, and approached them. He smiled as he came near and placed his hands, one on each of their heads. His voice was both soft and strong as he said, *"My beloved, I anoint you, Jack, and you, Laura, as my Sword-Bearers and High Priests for the Crossfire Team in the battle against evil on the Earth. I grant you understanding and wisdom in your efforts. You will be strong and courageous in my love for my Father's children and mighty in my holy anger against all the enemies of Heaven and Earth."*

The King of Kings lifted them to their feet and hugged them both as he said, *"I love you with a love everlasting."*

Jack felt the absolute perfection of the Universe in that moment and knew that it would never, ever leave him.

The Heavenly realm faded from view with the softness of velvet and an energy high that empowered them both.

Jack stopped outside the War Room and looked at Laura, I feel so full of love, enthusiasm, energy, direction, and desire to accomplish everything I have ahead of me. How do you feel?"

Laura looked inward and said, "All that and very clean and monumentally blessed."

Jack grinned, "WOW!"

As they walked into the War Room hand in hand, most of the Core Team was there and the happy look that appeared on their faces as Jack and Laura entered impacted Jack with a sense of gratitude and happiness.

Sarah got up and walked over to them and Mark followed her. Sarah stopped a pace away and smiled the most beautiful smile Jack had ever seen on her face. She simply said "Pray for me, please." That statement was echoed by the rest of the team as they clustered together behind Sarah and Mark.

Jack sensed the rightness of this request at this time. He recalled the feeling he had when Yahshua had hugged them and he knew he could pass that on to these people. He held out his hands and the eight people joined hands in a circle with Laura and him. He prayed out of a heart that yearned to pass the love of Yahshua on to them. "Father Yahveh, in the mighty Name of Your Son Yahshua, I anoint these people as Your faithful servants and warriors. Give them Your unlimited love and a connection with You that will never end. We love and honor each and every one of these children of Yours Father, as we know You love us all. Make them mighty in battle and worthy to lead our team to Your victory in Your Name. Amen."

Jack had felt the power flowing through him and Laura and then out through their hands to everyone in the circle. Four of them fell gently to the floor under the anointing and power of God. The other four were staggered but stayed on their feet. Jack turned to Laura and saw the golden glow of God on her face and the peace of God in her eyes.

CHAPTER THIRTY-SEVEN

Jack had finally gotten to sit down and relax just as Carol ran into the War Room. "I've got two Tel Aviv assignments off of the Matrix for demons to be in our dimension very soon. One group is near the Portal above us and includes four demons. The other one is close to where Tamar Moreh is now living. There is some kind of indication that Tamar's ex-husband, Shimon Ketzlya, is involved with these demons. There will be three demons in this group."

Laura shook her head, "Legal demons, we can't know how many illegal ones with be with either group."

There was a strong annunciation double tone throughout the Crossfire Team side of the Sea Base. Crayton's computer voice said, "There are indications that there are roughly eighteen demons and an unknown number of humans near the Portal.

The double tone sounded again. "There are indications of approximately seven demons in the area of Tamar Moreh's dwelling."

Jack's cell phone rang and he answered it. "Jack, this is Elon. I have police reports of demonic activity near the Portal and in the city. Can your team respond to these incursions?"

Jack told Elon that they would send their version of two flying teams to both locations. Elon said that the Mossad was also responding to both actions. Jack hung up and announced to the people in the War Room, "Everybody in the world is aware that there are demons in Tel Aviv." Laura hit the All-Team Members Alarm button and headed for the Armory to get her combat gear on. Jack was two steps behind her. They quickly put on their body armor and grabbed their weapons. They did this in the midst of the majority of the rest of the team doing the same thing. Jack looked around and told Laura it was just like getting ready for a high school football game in the locker room.

Jack hadn't seen Mark or Sarah in the Armory but they showed up in full gear and gave assignments to the troops.

When they got to Jack and Laura, Mark pointed out Core Team members and SOG members for the Malones to lead. He then said to Jack, "I will take the bigger party at the Portal. You guys save Eli's sister. David will know where."

Both teams ran to one of two Osprey Tilt Rotor aircraft and boarded. Ethan Reaper was moving them by aircraft in a small attempt to indicate that they weren't based below the Portal. Jack felt led to pray a blessing over the mixed IDF and Crossfire troops in both aircraft. He felt the Holy Spirit's presence and prayed, "Father Yahveh, we praise Your Mighty Name and petition You for Your protection. We ask that Your Holy Spirit be our guide and our shield over our lives and our protection in the coming battles."

Mark called him, "Jack, stay in prayer for all of us. This is probably a trap laid by the big ugly guy. He knows he's going to get his hand slapped for using demons illegally in the human dimension so he is drawing us out to get at us. Be wary."

Jack sat in his seat and prayed for wisdom concerning these two actions by Satan or at least by the demons. "Father Yahveh, I know that You denied Satan any more schemes where demons who You did not give permission to were not to cross into the human dimension. He has again exceeded his rights and sent illegal demons into our dimension causing us to leave the Sea Base and defend the innocent. Mark and I agree that these incursions are simply a trap designed to bring us out of the protected Sea Base. I definitely feel that we need to defend the people being threatened by these incursions but do not understand why this is being done. What is the motive or unseen things that the enemy of all mankind is to use against us? I ask this in Yahshua's name."

Jack waited for an answer but heard or felt nothing. The soldier next to him bumped him with his elbow which broke his concentration. He looked sternly at the body armor-clad warrior next to him on his left. This was a mixed troop with Crossfire Team and Mossad and IDF soldiers in the aircraft. Jack thought that he knew the man and then realized it was Raquel. It was no great reach for Jack to realize that the Archangel was his answer to his prayer.

Raquel nodded to Jack and leaned down to speak quietly to him. "Satan found a way for some of his demon swords or knives to slip through the protection of the Armor of God that your team has been anointed to use. God has determined what Satan found out and is changing the Armor so that Satan's advantages will no longer work. Take advantage of the fact that in their eagerness to use their swords that they now think will kill your people, they will become even sloppier than before and will leave themselves open to easy counter attack. Your advantage will be temporary so take advantage quickly."

Jack asked, "What did Satan find out? I thought that all demons, including him, weren't creative or innovative."

Raquel nodded, "They are not creative but they have studied us, the angels, as long as they have studied humans. Also, they understand how the effects of other dimensions play into operations in this dimension. One of the demons, the one Ethan Reaper called "Napoleon", saw that the energy field that God uses to empower the Armor, varies during a battle. He determined that if a demon could strike a team member when the field was weak there was a good chance that the demonic blade would not be stopped by the Armor. The demons can sense the power of the field of the Armor. It seems that Napoleon was able to show some other demons how to time their strikes when the Armor's field was at its weakest."

Jack asked how that was being overcome. Raquel shook his head. "That is beyond my understanding. I simply know that God has increased the amount of "Him" in the Armor so much that the armor can never again be penetrated by a demon blade."

Jack relayed that information to Mark. While he was talking he noticed that Raquel had unbuckled his seat belt and stood up. He walked down the aircraft and began to talk to one of the IDF troops sitting on the other side of the aircraft. Their conversation became heated and Raquel changed into his angelic warrior being and drew his sword. With one downward stroke he cut the head and chest of the man almost in two pieces.

The troops on both sides of the action had gotten up when the argument escalated and moved away. When the Archangel appeared they moved even farther away with looks of disbelief on their faces as the sword was used. A dozen troops looked back at Jack and David for help. But, by then the demon had been exposed and things settled down. However, none of the standing troops wanted to return to their seats and Jack could understand that.

Jack had been dismayed at first by Raquel's actions but after he watched as the man's body dissipated into ugly gray smoke and demon stain, he understood. Raquel faded out of sight only to reappear next to Jack as a trooper again.

Jack tapped the Archangel on the arm and thanked him. Then he asked, "What was that?"

Raquel stared at Jack for several seconds and then said, "demonic spy."Jack narrowed his eyes and said slightly sarcastically, "Are the rest of us in here okay?" Raquel nodded his head.

Jack got up and in a loud voice explained the event to the troops and got them to settle down. He returned to his seat and absolutely could not think of a single thing to say to Raquel. Jack knew that the Archangel had done what he did because it had to be done and Jack couldn't chastise him for it. Actually, Jack wasn't sure that he had the right to even question him about it.

CHAPTER THIRTY-EIGHT

After Jack's terse call about the demonic spy, Mark prayed and asked Yahshua to show him if there were any demons on his aircraft. He got the leading that everything was all right on his plane.

Mark's Osprey quickly flared out of horizontal flight and settled to the street with the rear ramp lowering as the plane reached the ground. Mark led the troops out and spread out as the Osprey lifted off and went to hover with the machine guns on the side facing the same direction as the troops. It then lifted higher and moved away from the troops as two Apache "Long Bow" attack helicopters dropped into the space the Osprey vacated. The Apaches could devastate tanks and obliterate ground forces with a vast array of weapons.

Mark used the battle communications to talk to Ethan in the COMSEC Department back in the Sea Base. "Talk to me Ethan. Where are these forces in the vicinity of the Portal?"

Ethan told Mark to check his battle ops. Mark slipped the eyepiece down over his left eye. He could see the location of the demons marked by the computer as swirling patterns on the eyepiece. The problem was, there was no sign of people and when Mark prayed his Armor did not appear. That didn't make sense. Too many sources had identified the fact that demons were in the area.

Mark called Jack who was having the same problem near Tamar's place; no enemy. Jack said, "Hold one."

Jack turned to Raquel. "Mark says that there are no people or demons near the Portal, either."

Raquel told Jack to wait a while as he faded out of sight. The Archangel reappeared in less than a minute. He was in his angelic form. He told Jack, "Do not go back to the Sea Base directly. This is a false lead to draw you out so that the RHONE forces can determine your base's location."

Jack relayed the information to Mark. Mark was irritated but at the same time he could see the devil's hand in this. He told Jack, "Satan cannot use his illegal entry of demons without incurring the Wrath of God. So he's found a way to fake a demon symbol to the Computer Center and other groups to pull us into Marco Marino's gun sights. I think I have an idea of how to make this backfire on Marino and Satan. Get your troops back onto the Osprey and head for the WMD plant in the Jordanian desert. I'll fill you in then."

Jack told the Apaches to return to the base and the Osprey to land again and take on the troops. He prayed for complete blockage of any demonic power to see, hear, or understand anything the two sets of troops were doing.

Mark did the same thing and then called Su Li and Mark White to his location. When they ran up he gave them specific instructions and they took off at a run. Mark loaded up with the other troops and they lifted off and headed toward Jordan.

Mark made a quick call to Ethan and then had Charlie Wu talk him through what Mark wanted.

As the two Ospreys flew nap of the Earth protocols, they penetrated Jordanian airspace. Mark brought Jack up to date on his plan.

Forty-five minutes later the Ospreys settled to the ground less than a mile from the secret Jordanian manufacturing plant and the troops disembarked. The Ospreys shut down and the pilots joined the ground forces.

Jack jogged over to Mark. "What does Ethan see?"

Mark reached over and swung down the eyepiece on Jack's helmet. Jack stared at the data and the numbers and stared at Mark with a look of disbelief. "How did you know about this?"

Mark grinned, "It's what I would have done if I was in charge of the RHONE.

There were rumblings and clanking and seemingly out of nowhere the desert started falling away from camouflaged tank and personnel positions. Jack counted at least twenty main battle tanks and over a thousand troops appearing from nowhere. Mark spoke into his combat microphone and said, "Now!"

Jack and Mark signaled the troops to drop to the ground.

The RHONE division was charging toward the fifty or so Crossfire troops and the two Ospreys as they opened fire.

Jack covered his head as the first shells hit the desert and destroyed one of the Osprey Tilt Rotor aircraft in a direct hit. He looked at Mark and yelled over the noise. "You _are_ aware that we don't have our Force Generators this time?"

Mark was about to reply when the skies opened up and twenty Israeli Air Force drones flashed overhead and unleashed too many missiles to count. Tanks exploded, entire groups of soldiers disappeared and most Bradley fighting vehicles were destroyed during the pass. As the drones flew away the anti-aircraft missiles and anti-aircraft batteries that were still functioning turned to try and knock the drones down.

That was when sixteen American-made A-10 "Wart Hogs" flew over the Crossfire Team, at the RHONE troops, using their 30mm Avenger Gatling guns, firing 4,200 high-explosive rounds per minute and laser-guided air-to-ground missiles, obliterated the enemy forces. The anti-aircraft batteries and missile launchers were pointed the wrong direction and it probably would not have mattered if they weren't because there was at least one missile for each battery. After the A-10s vacated the area, three MK-84, 2,000 pound Joint Directed Munitions (JDAM) bombs fell at the back of the attacking force and literally obliterated anything left of the command and control forces for the RHONE. These had come from Israeli Air Force bombers flying at six thousand feet above the battlefield.

The JDAM bombs were almost three quarters of a mile away from the Crossfire troops but still bounced them around from the sheer force of the explosions.

Jack was trying to get his eyesight and hearing back to normal when Mark said, "That might get the RHONE'S attention and possibly keep them from messing with us for a while."

Jack had to agree with his friend. He looked over the cratered and smoking battlefield where there had been close to two thousand troops. Nothing was left standing or moving or alive. It was a massively accurate picture of what war was about.

Jack sighed, "I wish we hadn't had to do that."

Mark said, "Jack, I prayed and that was what the Father said to do. This was another unapproved aggression by Satan using the anti-Christ's little army of the RHONE. You know that I could not have gotten that kind of reaction out of the Israeli Military no matter how many times we've saved them from destruction. It would have taken weeks just to get this coordinated air strike in a foreign country approved by the government. This was an ongoing plan already in operation. I just offered to be the bait and lure them out of their secret hiding place. You see, thanks to Satan and his demons, the RHONE expected us to drop in. They believed Ethan's phony email that this is the site of our base and they sent their second group to destroy it. Their first group was an exploratory force to ensure we were really here and it happened while David's group was escorting Ethan to send the email from here."

"I had contacted the IDF to tell them that we were going to head out to the Jordanian secret WMD base to throw the RHONE off again. They confided in me that they were already geared up to stop this RHONE attack because they had been instructed by God to do it. I just offered to help start the war and the Israeli Military didn't waste the opportunity. They did this to help their neighbors, the Jordanians, defeat an unknown and hostile force. Guess who personally told the IDF that God commanded them to attack this force? It was none less than Rabbi Simon ben Chanan! He and the Prime Minister got the unanimous agreement of the Kinnesit."

Jack silently thanked the Father in Heaven for arranging the whole thing and weaving them into it, through the Rabbi who had his eyes opened to the demonic forces in the world, when he had come to speak with the team to learn what they were really about. Jack remembered thinking after the attack by a really bad demon that the Rabbi now had an up close and personal understanding of their business.

Jack shook his head and was about to order their troops to confirm the lethality of the attack by walking the battlefield and seeing if anyone was still alive out there when his cell phone chirped. Jack answered the phone and heard the voice of General Sayif of the Jordanian Army. "How are you, General Sayif?"

The General felt indebted to Jack for saving him from demons several weeks ago in this same area of the desert. "I am fine General Malone. I hear you are back and killing people this time instead of demons."

Jack explained the battle and what led up to it. The General seemed to already know some of it and was very pleased that the RHONE had just been summarily evicted from his land. "I applaud you and your Israeli allies in your victory. If you would please leave the area now I will have my men search the area for any RHONE troops that may have survived, although I doubt we will find anyone alive after that battle. You are part of the reason I now have to reconstruct my office. Those last three bombs reorganized it and then destroyed it. I can now understand the use of them and I am glad that they weren't aimed at us."

Jack asked him how he was managing with his superiors after he had taken Christ as his Savior.

The General coughed twice and then asked Jack, "Please do not speak of that since it is such a personal thing to me."

Jack understood the General's predicament. He had helped to engineer a similar situation for God in China recently.

CHAPTER THIRTY-NINE

Jack had a thought and decided to follow up on it. He reached out and tapped Mark's arm as he was describing the battle to someone on the phone. "Mark, when you get a minute..."

Mark finished his conversation and said, "Thank you, Mr. Prime Minister. Yes, Sir! I will, Sir. Goodbye." He disconnected the call and looked at Jack. "What do you need, buddy?"

Jack said, "I think I got a message from above and we need to act on it right now. Contact Ethan and have him bounce a message off of your phone or mine so it looks like it came from here. Have him send a message to that free offer from the RHONE to reward whoever tells them where the Crossfire Team has their base. If it is still working and I'm pretty sure it will be, the message is this. "Try to remember, you are not fighting us, You're fighting the living God that created the Universe and you can never win." Sign it, The Crossfire Team."

Mark grinned, "That should just about frost them. I'm sure they're looking at satellite videos of the "battle" right now and are trying to figure out how we were able to get the Israeli help in time. They are probably beginning to wonder who the mole is in their organization. God said our battles would begin to rot the wood of their organization and kill them from the inside out." He contacted Ethan and told him what to do.

Jack waited until Mark hung up and told him that the day wasn't over yet. Mark studied Jack's face. "You've been talking to Abba again, haven't you?"

Jack realized he'd been praying while Mark set up the message. But for him to have a glow from prayer rather than in person? "I have been praying and there is one more little thing God wants us to do before we call it a day."

Mark smiled. "And that one little more thing would be?"

"We need to go back to where we were and finish the job we started today. Satan is using both of these events as diversions to ensure that he can actually do what he started to do in Tel Aviv."

Mark looked at the smoking ruin of one of the Tilt Rotor aircraft. "We've only got one bus, boss."

Jack shook his head as he grinned back at him. "I think our ride is here."

Mark looked up and saw the X-76, now called the "Ghost" by its designers, dropping to the sand near them. "Nice ride. Do we need the speed so we can cover both places?"

Jack nodded as a second "Ghost" landed next to the first one. Mark smiled as he keyed his battle microphone. "Load 'em up right now. We have the same distribution and the same destinations as this morning."

As the team split up and ran to the UAVs, Laura asked, "I wondered what those big bills for the line item "research" were going to produce. Why are we going back to Tel Aviv? Aren't we supposed to be throwing the RHONE off the scent? Won't they see these UAVs and wonder about them?"

Jack concentrated on running with his gear as he answered her. "Yes, that was what the "research" bills were for, but, we only paid for thirty percent of the cost. Victor covered the rest. And he wants to ride on both, one of these and the Shrew, too. He's paid for them and I guess he can ride anytime he wants to. We are going back to stop the demon attack on the Portal and Tamar that were given to us as a phony deal this morning. The way Raquel tells it, the demons were able to show us them massing this evening, only earlier in the morning. Something about no time for them lets them move things around. We are going to finish off these attacks and then vanish from their view. Lastly, they won't see the UAVs, either here or there. Raquel says that they don't exist for the enemy."

They had reached the doorway into the first Ghost and climbed aboard. The door closed as they sat down and belted in.

The forward Vision Screen showed the quick lift off as the craft turned toward Tel Aviv. The world under them accelerated and shrank rapidly and the altitude and speed indicators showed them lifting to six miles in altitude and moving up to 3,000 miles per hour, briefly. Then the Ghost almost stopped forward flight and dropped faster than a rock straight down. The city of Tel Aviv grew in the Vision Screen and then became the same street scene they landed on with the Osprey that morning.

As the Ghost landed, Jack said in a command voice. "Lock and Load, ladies and gentlemen, this time you get to fight."

There was a cheer that filled the aircraft. The troops exited the aircraft quickly and it lifted away silently.

Jack and Laura moved up the street past Tamar's apartment and started praying. Two more steps and their armor and swords and shields appeared. Demons began to emerge into the human dimension and the rifle shots the four-man repression team laid on them, cut their numbers by more than half. Jack felt that Holy Anger building in him again and he headed for the demons that didn't die.

Jack met the first rank of demons and killed the first three before a black sword even hit his armor. He went into High Speed Time Management and took out four more demons. He saw a flash of gold as a demon that tried to jump on his back was sent to the pit by Laura and her sword. There were four other sword bearers on the field besides him. Laura, Su Li, Alexis and Megan were mighty in their golden armor and David was in silver like himself.

Three demons tried to tackle Jack and bind him but he used his training in Martial Arts to jump over the one trying for his legs and cut the head off of a second one. The third one ran directly into him which sent him tumbling to the ground. This is one of the specialties of a Jui Jitsu follower. Jack spun around on his back in time to shove his sword through the demon still on the ground and take a direct hit on his chest armor with a black blade. That blade slid off of the armor and brought the last of the three face to face with Jack. Jack couldn't say anything about the demon's breath or his lack of dental hygiene but could bring his shining sword up between the demon's legs and split him all the way up until he hit the demon's chest.

Jack rolled to his left in time to get hit by a demon's kick. He immediately went back into the Time Compression, High Speed mode. That slowed down the next attack by a large demon which was already in the air to land on him. Jack went to his knees and struck upward with his sword. The blade gleaming with the power of Yahveh cleaved the air-borne demon into two smaller, yet non-functional, parts. Jack immediately threw his blade into a horizontal block behind his head. That deflected the demon blade that was coming down at that self-same head. Jack spun around on his knees and cut the demon behind him in half.

That gave Jack the chance he needed to rise to his feet and spin in a circle with his blade held out in a circle to cut and slice two more demons. He moved toward clear space to get more combat room when he saw a golden set of armor on the ground several feet away from his position. Instead of fear, the Holy Anger within him went into overload maximum and he started slicing and dicing every demon he came near as he worked his way over to the fallen female warrior. He knew she wasn't dead or unconscious because the armor was still evident.

He got to the warrior on the ground and he cleared a wide circle in the demons around her. He stepped forward and reached down with his left hand to the hand the fallen warrior raised as Jack swung his sword in an arc to back off two things that looked like Orcs out of the Fellowship of the Ring movies. Pulling mightily, he pulled the warrior up onto her feet and she ran a demon behind Jack through. They went back-to-back and continued to slay demons. There was a black blade shoved at Jack but the woman leaned forward and the blade went between their backs. Jack back-handed the head off of the demon the sword belonged to and went back to high guard position only to find that the dissolving demon was the last of the bunch. He stepped forward and stopped praying and his armor and sword disappeared.

Jack turned around and found Alexis holding her side and bleeding from a wound that had gotten past her armor somehow. Jack immediately put his hand over the wound and started praying. As he prayed he felt the heaviness that he felt whenever the Holy Spirit was near and attentive to their requests. "Father Yahveh, I ask in the Name of Your Son, Yahshua, that You heal Your faithful daughter who has fought valiantly for Your Glory and Honor. And I declare with Yahshua's stripes, this warrior daughter of Yours is healed." It is in Yahshua's Mighty

Name we ask that all sickness, illness, curses, and enemy poison is removed from her body and she is healed, and healed completely. It is in Yahshua's Name we pray for this healing."

He took his hand away from her side and checked her wound. There was nothing to see and there was no blood on his hand, either. He prayed loudly, "All Praise be given to the Almighty Yahveh and His Son Yahshua!"

He was suddenly hugged by Alexis who was crying out of her happiness and relief after being healed completely. All of the other warriors arrived where Jack stood with Alexis' arms around his neck. He slowly turned his head and found Laura next to him with her hand on Alexis' back.

David showed up and smiled at the sight of the three of them standing there together. Alexis took a deep breath and stepped back from Jack. She smiled at Laura as David put his arms around her. She snuggled into his embrace and started crying softly as she told him about the wound and Jack's prayer.

Jack looked around and asked if anyone else had been wounded. No one raised a hand or asked for prayer.

Jack hugged Laura and asked if she or anyone else knew if Tamar and her children were all right. Laura nodded her head. "I sent Megan to defend her and she did. Only five demons got to the floor of her apartment and none of them got to Tamar or the kids. Megan is still with her."

Jack looked around and prayed but his armor didn't appear. He asked a general question. "Did any of you see any people that were supposed to be involved in this assault?"

Su Li raised her hand. "There was only one human on the demon's side and he led the demons to Tamar's place. One demon stayed with him as the others busted down the door to the apartment building. They ran into Megan. I took out the demon and while I was battling the demon the man shot at me six times with a revolver. My armor deflected all of the shots and I cut the man down with my sword when he charged me with a knife. It was Tamar's ex-husband."

Jack noted that the Tel Aviv police had arrived on the scene and were being filled in by one of the Mossad troops. Jack realized that it was Elon.

CHAPTER FORTY

An Osprey, piloted by Su Li, landed behind them, and lowered its ramp The troops loaded on board and more or less collapsed into their seats for the short ride home to the Sea Base since there were no snooping satellites in position to see them.

Later, Jack and Laura were relaxing in their apartment when the door chime sounded. Jack checked the monitor and saw that it was David and Alexis. He pushed the button on the console and the couple came in and sat down. David smiled at two of his best friends in the world. If it hadn't been for them, he'd still be training new agents at the Mossad, would never have killed a demon, and most of all he never would have met Yahshua and the beautiful woman sitting next to him. He looked at Jack and Laura and asked, "How are you two getting along?"

Jack grinned, "We're great, what's up with you two?"

Alexis sat up. "Guys, we have a lead on who and what your "Napoleon" is. This is based upon what we learned from Carol. There appear to be a few "Napoleons" that show up every now and then. It is an anomaly in the demon ranks. A demon that is deformed and ugly from its time with Satan. But, it retains more of its centuries old ex-angel intelligence. It hasn't been reduced to an almost mindless beast that is fit for no more than to be destroyed like most of them that we meet. The Napoleon's problem is that Satan hates them. Anything that has intelligence to do things other than what it's been told to do."

"Since we can't comb the demonic portion of the spiritual dimension to find him, we thought that we should lure him out to where we can send him on his way to the pit."

Jack shrugged, "Yeah, kicking in doors in the demonic section might take a lot more firepower than we have. Okay, how do you suggest we "lure" him out of his dimension?"

David said, "He seems to be around in our world whenever there is a battle with our team lately. Why don't we create a mini-team that can break off from the main battle and focus on taking him out?"

Jack nodded, "Get Ethan to do an ID kit on Napoleon so that the new "Mini-Team" will know who he is. I think that we will have more battles pretty soon. Since the four of us are usually in the thick of things, why don't we make Ethan, Megan, and Carol the Mini-Team? You know, let them work the fringes of the battle and watch for their target?

Laura spoke up. "On another matter, I would like to see about getting Ms. Twinkle Toes here to work with everyone to be more like her when battling demons. If you watch the last battle you will see that she makes the demons miss more than hit."

Jack looked at Alexis, "Do you want to teach us some of your movements?"

Alexis shrugged, "I can probably show the women how to do what I do, but I'm not too sure about the guys. This takes a certain feminine body carriage and hip movement that most guys aren't good at."

David threw in, "Yeah, but still we would really like to watch anyway."

Alexis smacked him on the arm, "Hey, hey!"

David went wide eyed and said, "Who, me?"

In the War Room Mark was trying to determine why a blade from the enemy could get through Alexis' armor after Raquel had told Jack that the armor was improved so that demonic blades could not penetrate it.

He had prayed and had not gotten an answer, an angel, a voice, nothing, not even a leading. He tried to determine what was different with that battle, Alexis' armor, or any other variable. His cell phone chirped and he looked at the caller ID window. It was Hiram Tzahal, Director of the Mossad. "Yes, Director, what can I do for you?"

The Director spoke softly, "Mark, I have a problem that may have a demonic element to it. I cannot be sure who to turn to because I think we have a traitor in the Mossad, or possibly in the Kidon. I received information about a major plan to attack Israel from the tunnels behind the Western Wall in Jerusalem. I know you and your team were there recently stopping a terrorist attempt to set off some nuclear weapons. I'm afraid that if I have anybody in the Mossad or the Kidon or even your team move to confirm this information, the mole, or moles will see the movement and the enemy will relocate the source of the attack."

Mark asked, "Where in the tunnels is this information?"

Hiram Tzahal sighed. "All I have is two tunnel locator numbers. I am concerned if I were to go there and verify the place I will be seen and killed or again, spook the holder of the information into running. I don't want you to be in any danger but if you can confirm that there is such a location then I can try some form of misdirection and get some troops there to raid the place. I'm sure that everyone on your team is trustworthy but you and David Zahavy are the only two I really know. David is too well known as a Mossad Agent from his earlier life to have him check it out. Can you do this for me? It must be "Eyes-Only" and bring the confirmation to me alone."

Mark said, "Could you hang on for a minute?"

After Hiram agreed to wait, Mark put the phone on hold and prayed about his involvement. "Father Yahveh, this prayer is for wisdom. The Director is asking me to help him at the risk of my being alone in Jerusalem to find out information for him. Is this something I should do or not?" He thought for a second. "I ask this in Yahshua's Name. Amen."

He waited and the only thing he felt was that there was no condemnation of this effort. He clicked back onto the line and asked Hiram for the location numbers for the tunnel system.

The Director gave Mark the numbers and swore him to complete secrecy, now and after the operation. Mark agreed and hung up.

Mark thought about the request and realized that Director Tzahal lived in a royally messed-up business. When you run a group like the Mossad and could only trust a newbie Israeli citizen to circumvent his own organization, that was sad.

After thinking about the secrecy angle Mark made a delayed phone call to Ethan and gave him the basic facts of the situation. He uploaded the message to a Cloud Server and shut his phone off. If everything worked out all right, he would be able to retrieve the message and erase it before it was sent.

He called Sarah and told her he had to do a clandestine task for the Director of Mossad and would be back that night around ten or eleven. He swore her to secrecy due to the sensitive nature of the request.

Sarah wasn't pleased but understood that Mark was honor-bound to help the Mossad Director after all the help he had given the team. She told Mark, "You need backup, let me come with you. The Director won't mind."

Mark knew she was right and decided to include her in the plan. "Okay, but we can't let everyone know what we're doing. I left a delayed phone message with Ethan and if anything delays us then the whole team will know." Sarah agreed with that. She ran down to the War Room and accompanied Mark out of the Sea Base. Mark told the security detail at the Portal that he and Sarah were going to Jerusalem to see a Rabbi that needed their help concerning demons.

The Portal guard remembered two friends of his that had been killed by a demon right here at the Portaland decided that he would let these experts handle the supernatural. He ordered them a car and checked them out at 11 A.M.

CHAPTER FORTY-ONE

Mark and Sarah covered the thirty-six miles in less than an hour and parked as close as possible to the Western wall in a parking lot. Dressed as tourists they walked down to the wall and looked at various things that had always interested them. Sarah was familiar with the wall from her youth and guided Mark to several booths and sales. After a half-hour of aimless wandering which brought them to the entrance to the tunnels behind the wall and under the Dome of the Rock, they bought tickets to individually tour the open tunnels.

Mark and Sarah had both memorized the numbers that Director Tzahal had given them and realized immediately that those numbers were not on the regular tour path. As an ex-Mossad Agent, Sarah took the lead and managed to avoid the tunnel cameras and still slide off of the routine tour path and enter into an unlit and uninhabited section of the tunnels. She was careful to check for infrared beams and cameras and adroitly circumnavigated all of them. Twice they had to hide from guards walking these tunnels.

Eventually they found the right combination of east-west and north-south numbers. Mark checked and found a definite room behind locked doors with the address.

He looked at Sarah and shrugged. "We found the address and there is a room for that address. I think we're done."

Sarah looked around. "There are no guards, cameras or other sensing devices in this part of the old tunnels where weare." She looked at Mark. "Do you think that driving all the way here and back just to locate a real building at the correct address is worthwhile? What if we just carefully took a look around inside to confirm the state of habitation and the possibility of a source of data before we leave?"

Mark was learning to lean on God rather than himself. He prayed, hard, and still did not get any answer. "Okay, but just a look, no internal investigation. It could blow any chance that the Mossad could find what they are looking for here."

Sarah looked at her husband. "I was a Mossad operative for years. I don't understand a request simply to confirm an address. There has to be more to it than that. We need to check it out."

Mark sighed and agreed. Sarah told him to watch for company while she worked on the door lock. Mark shrank back into the alcove-like entrance and watched for any guards.

Sarah was sure she was right when she found a brand new padlock on the door rather than the old style door lock. She used her tools and had the lock open in less than a minute. She tapped Mark and he slipped the lock out of the hasp it was in and set it to the side. He slowly turned the door handle and opened the door. It was pitch black inside and he turned on his Nightfighter flashlight. It showed a dirty floor covered in undisturbed dust with cobwebs and a really musty smell.

He didn't go in but checked out the status of the room carefully from the doorway. Sarah stood behind him and checked it out also. There were no signs anyone had been there for a long, long time. He stepped back and closed the door gently. He replaced the padlock and turned to go. Sarah stepped out of the alcove and looked all four ways. There was no one there. She turned to tell Mark but he wasn't there either. She turned on her flashlight and saw his footprints in the dust in the alcove. They stopped right behind her. She sighed and stepped to the back of the alcove and ran her light around the entire area of the alcove. No doors, nothing.

At this point a normal woman would run off to find help or summon the authorities. Sarah was a trained spy, assassin, and warrior. She squatted down and looked at the dust where Mark's footprints were. She could see that the dust to the left was somewhat smeared whereas the dust on the right wasn't. That told her that Mark's feet moved to the left after he had stepped at that point. She remembered hearing a noise but thought it was Mark's feet walking on the metal grate in the floor of the alcove.

She brought out her phone and made six close-up pictures of the footprints and the alcove. She was sure that Mark had been taken in some form of trap.

Sarah heard voices approaching her position. She turned out the flashlight and moved away from the voices. She found an even better alcove twenty feet from the place they had entered. She faded out of sight and waited until the two guards had walked past the two alcoves and disappeared down the tunnel.

Once she was alone she decided that they needed help, big time. She checked and her phone had two bars. Enough to get a phone call out. She dialed the Sea Base and Ethan answered the call. "Yes, Sarah, what can I do for you?" Sarah started to tell Ethan the problem when her cell phone was knocked out of her hand and busted on the floor of the tunnel.

Sarah started to pray and her golden armor and the Sword of the Word explosively appeared and lit up the tunnels. Sarah stepped to her right and executed a series of strikes behind her and in front of her position. The fact that her armor appeared meant there was at least one demon in her vicinity. She prayed that the Father would give her discernment and wisdom to defeat the enemy. Suddenly she saw five demons angling to grab her and strike her. Her Holy Anger went from hot to white hot.

CHAPTER FORTY-TWO

Mark had just turned and taken one step behind Sarah when he felt paralyzed and couldn't speak. The metal grate of the alcove detached and silently swung open, dropping him down twenty or thirty feet. He knew the grate had swung shut again because Sarah's light disappeared from his vision. He couldn't move and struck the bottom of the shaft. He hit with his feet hard. He thought it would knock him out but it didn't. Something he couldn't see grabbed him and pulled him backward into what he considered would be the basement of the house they'd found.

It was still pitch black as the force holding him moved him along. He could feel the breeze on his neck as the dank air passed. He prayed for God's help but still nothing. He was perfectly awake and sensed everything, he just couldn't move anything.

A light source behind him began to make things visible and got brighter as he moved toward the light. A few minutes passed as he was lifted through a doorway and pulled on heavy floor tiles to a position somewhere in the middle of whatever room he was in. He felt unseen hands searching his pockets. He felt his gun and his knife, plus his cell phone taken from him. The unseen, but stinky force, that had moved him stood him upright and left him. Several seconds later the door slammed shut with a sound that meant it was very thick and solid.

All at once his paralysis left him and he almost fell. He caught himself and looked around. He was in a square room, roughly thirty feet by thirty feet and probably fifteen feet high. The light was indirect from a sconce near the ceiling. There was no furniture or anything in the room except him. Understanding that this was enemy action and he was fairly certain that the nasty breath of whatever invisible force pulled him into the room was a demon. He started evaluating whatever forces or advantages he had. Basically, Mark decided that he had nothing except himself and his spirit to battle whatever was coming. He recognized the décor and setting as a dramatic setup. He was pretty sure he knew who was behind this elaborate charade to capture him. Mark knew his ultimate fate and wasn't worried about dying. Well, maybe the method of dying could be worrisome, but the eventual destination was assured. So let's get the show on the road.

He decided that he would aggravate his captor to start with and perhaps he could make it make a mistake out of uncontrolled anger. He said, "You know I have more important things to do than just amuse you."

The voice that answered him was a very familiar cold and evil one he'd heard a few days ago as he had destroyed Moloch. "Shut Up Worm! You will talk when I tell you to and not say anything else!"

Mark yawned, "Is that the best you can come up with?"

Mark expected pain throughout his body or something equally gruesome. Instead all he got was silence. So he crossed his legs and sat down on the floor. "At least you could provide a chair for your guest. You're a horrible host."

The voice came back with a sense of humor of its own. "You know I can just leave you there until you die of thirst."

Mark came back with, "Please, that would be a better than you talking me to death."

The dead voice said, "Let me tell you what I am going to do with you. The first thing you need to understand is that you are completely in my power. This room has always been exclusively mine. Your misbegotten angels and even your god himself cannot come into this room to save you because he gave his word that he would never do that. As you are fond of saying, "god will not break his own word or then he wouldn't be god."

"Your puny armor and sword cannot be activated in this room because it has to be connected to your puny god to work. Not even his essence can enter here. There is no hope for you. You will die the way I want you to repay me for the losses you caused me. And you can be assured I will drag it out for a long, long time. You will suffer a thousand deaths before your body is thrown out as it rots into the dung heaps of Jerusalem."

Mark shook his head. "There you go again, trying to talk me to death. I can assure you of one thing, Satan. My death and suffering will be a trillion times shorter than yours in the Lake of Fire. Those "misbegotten angels" will be there to watch you suffer and ensure that you will suffer terribly for all eternity. I have no pity for you and when you have endured all that you can stand there will still be the rest of eternity ahead of you. Of course, you know you deserve it."

Mark realized that he may have hit a nerve there. The lights flickered somewhat and then a demon appeared in the room. It was your typical ugly as sin demon and it was armed with one of those black swords.

The voice came back oily and smooth. "Your death will silence you and then I will bring your wife in here while your mangled body is still lying there. She may be more contrite than you are."

Mark studied the demon as he stood up and spoke. "You obviously don't understand women and if you think I'm trouble, you wait. She'll bring heaven down on your little operation here."

The demon ran at Mark with death in its eyes and the sword raised on high. Mark started to pray his battle prayer, not expecting his armor and sword to appear and they didn't. He prayed because he knew God could hear him even if the present tenant owned the property. He evaluated the attack of the demon and responded as he would for a big and really, really ugly human being.

The demon brought the sword downward in an arc designed to cut Mark into two pieces. Mark stepped inside of the arc of the sword and slammed his right fist into the throat of the demon with everything he had from the heel of his right foot and every muscle he could all the way to his fist. The demon outweighed him by probably a hundred pounds but, still it was based on a human or angel structure and it had the same weak spots. As he stepped forward and drove his right fist into the demon's throat the forward motion of the demon only added to the impact on its throat.

Mark heard the sudden "Crack" of the larynx as the demon's head snapped back from the force of the punch. Mark then turned to his left, throwing his right fist to his left he then rotated back to his right and put every bit of his energy and body torque into a right elbow strike to the right temple area of the demon's head. This only stunned the demon where it would have completely killed a normal human being.

The beast could not get a breath into its lungs because of the crushed larynx and Mark took full advantage of its incapacity by jumping up and coming down with a devastating right side kick to the demon's right knee. This broke the knee joint and sent the choking demon to the floor. It dropped the sword to reach for its neck.

Mark picked up the sword and executed the demon by cutting its head off of its body. He dropped the demonic sword as it began to turn into smoke along with its owner. Mark then walked away from the demon stain and stood quietly waiting for the next, and probably nastier, executioner. He figured he would keep it up while he could and then give the next one an open path to strike him dead. It would be a quick way to go to God and deprive Satan of his victory.

CHAPTER FORTY-THREE

Up in the tunnels above the room Mark was in; Sarah stepped forward and immediately went into the Time Compression, High Speed technique that Hugo had taught her. She killed all five of the demons before they could react. They dissipated slowly in the tunnel and the lights were dimmed for a distance in all directions. This did little to subdue her Holy Anger for she was mad, very mad.

She picked up her cell phone but it was beyond working, smashed completely. Sarah's armor and sword disappeared even though she was still praying.

Sarah called softly, "Raquel." "You said that you would be here if we needed you. Please attend to my prayer because my husband is lost and in the hands of Satan."

The tunnels were still dark and quiet. Sarah prayed that Yahveh would help her. She sighed but did not resort to tears. The anger, hers and the Holy Anger were fueling her at this point and she decided to get into the building one way or the other.

All she needed was a pound of C4 explosive and a timer. Then, a quiet voice said, "Sarah, you can have a violent nature about you at times."

Sarah spun around and saw Raquel standing there. Before she could say anything the Archangel said, "I know."

Sarah looked at the angel. "Is there anything you can do to save Mark?"

He was quiet for several seconds and then nodded. "No, but together we can possibly save him." Raquel let Sarah see Mark as he was. She saw the demon stain and Mark quietly standing there, obviously waiting for the next "thing" to appear.

Raquel said, "I cannot enter that space because God granted it to Satan for all time and expressly forbid any angels or even Himself from entering or interfering with what goes on there. It has been that way for two thousand, five hundred years. But, I think you have a solution. Stay here."

Raquel was back in twenty seconds. He handed Sarah a package. She opened the package and found one pound of C4 explosive and a timer. "Set the timer and tell me where to hold it." Sarah looked at him with concern. "Will the explosion hurt you?"

Raquel shook his head. "No, I'm a legal spirit, bullets and bombs don't affect me. Show me where and an outside view of the room Mark was in appeared in the air in front of Sarah and she pointed at the door into the room. "About five feet back from the door should blow the door into the room. But, it might knock Mark out from the blast."

Raquel said, "Then you will have to go in there and bring him out. I cannot go into the room."

Sarah nodded, "Here I've set it for thirty seconds."

Raquel took the package and drew his sword. He smashed it down on the metal grate and jumped into the hole which appeared. Sarah moved back to the next tunnel opening and waited.

The explosion shook dust down from everywhere and made her dance to stay up. She ran back to the shaft and looked down it. Raquel stepped out and told her to jump. Sarah trusted Raquel and simply stepped out over the opening and dropped into the angel's arms. He put her on the ground and she ran down the hall to the area of where the door once was. She climbed over the debris and walked into the room. She saw the demon stain, but she didn't see Mark. She called out to him. "Mark! Are you all right?"

From behind her, Mark said. "Hi sweetie, I see you found me."

He smiled at her and she took his hand and they ran for the door. They both got out of the door and ran to the bottom of the shaft. The walls were smooth and there was no way to climb the thirty feet to the top.

There was a lot of noise behind them and a waft of putrid air came out of the hall. Sarah put her hand on Mark's chest and stepped forward praying her battle prayer and her armor and sword appeared. She stepped into the hall and saw a horrid sight. This demon was the result of several botched medical experiments and possibly a really large blender. It didn't resemble a human in any way. But it had many arms and swords and it moved on something that looked like fleshy tracks.

Sarah didn't know where to attack it. She was about to just start quartering it when there was a flash of light, power, energy, electricity or something that completely fried the thing. It started to dissipate when there was a blast that came from above where Mark stood. They ran to the other end of the tunnel and turned to look up.

There was no alcove any longer, just a big hole. Mark looked at Sarah and up at the remnants of the alcove. "See what happens when you give new toys to the angels."

Raquel appeared next to Mark. "Here, perhaps this will destroy Satan's space. He handed Mark four pounds of C4 and a timer.

Mark said, "This much explosive will kill Sarah and I if we are in this hall or shaft."

Raquel said, "Set the timer for ten seconds and I will get you out of here."

Mark did as he was asked. Then he turned and pitched the charge into the room and yelled, "Satan, remember the Lake of Fire? Fire in the hole!!"

Raquel took hold of them both and flew them out of the hole and all the way to the edge of the authorized tunnel path. The C4 went off and it was only a heavy rumble and solid shaking where they were. Raquel disappeared and Sarah looked at Mark. He didn't have a scratch on him that she could see. "WOW! Buddy, you still know how to show a girl a good time."

Mark sighed. "Well possibly not this time. I think I said some things that angered the big ugly guy. We'd better get home while we can."

An hour later they walked into the War Room to find it full of activity. Mark asked Jack, "What's up?"

Jack looked at them and said, "It seems the lost has been found. Crayton spotted you coming into the base."

There were cheers and Jack eyed the demon stain on Mark's clothes. He shook his head. "I'm almost afraid to ask. But, where have you two been?"

After Mark and Sarah told their stories as After-Action reports, Jack brought them up to date on the home scene. "First, Director Tzahal of the Mossad is recuperating from a nasty gash on his head. He has no idea of who hit him but he remembers a dream where he was talking to Mark about a tunnel. We can now straighten him out on what happened to him. Second, the security detail here at the Portal says that somebody keyed the car they loaned you and they want you to pay to fix it up. Thirdly, Ethan had his first panic attack when Sarah called with something urgent and then her phone died, Mark's medallion couldn't be found on the entire planet and Sarah's medallion was somewhere under the Western Wall in Jerusalem."

Sarah laughed, "A quiet explanation should put him back in order. He might now have a real understanding of some of the pressures of the job."

Jack asked, "Why didn't either of you call after you headed back?"

Mark shrugged his shoulders, "My phone was fried by Satan and hers was broken by five demons.

Laura looked at her best friend. "You took on five demons at once by yourself?

Sarah grinned, "Yeah, they didn't have a chance."

Jack shook his head and the looked at Mark. "You killed a demon without your armor or sword? Really?"

Mark shrugged his shoulders again. "I didn't have much of a choice, now did I? The demon just thought he had all the advantage. Stupid demon."

Jack asked if either of them needed prayer after their ordeal.

Mark looked at Sarah and then said, "Why not? The big ugly guy was talking to me and he could have cursed me again."

Jack and Laura prayed that any curses or assignments against Mark and Sarah be removed and burned up in the fire of the Holy Spirit. This time Jack felt led to pray over Mark's ears.

CHAPTER FORTY-FOUR

As they finished praying for Mark and Sarah, Raquel appeared. Jack welcomed the Archangel and asked him what he thought of Satan's room in the Western Wall tunnels.

Raquel smiled at the four humans. "When will Satan learn not to irritate Mark? There is no Satan's Room there anymore. The blast brought down the roof and a considerable amount of rock, approximately two hundred tons. Even though we were not allowed to enter that space there was no agreement that we couldn't destroy that space from the outside as we did."

Mark asked, "Raquel, I was surprised when Satan stopped talking to me and the fact that he never sent a second demon to attack me. Can you tell me why that was?"

Raquel nodded his head. "Yes. Once again Satan overstepped one of his agreements with God. He used a demon that did not have God's approval to attack and use Director Tzahal of the Mossad to mislead Mark. He also used a demonic covering over you so that your prayers could not reach Heaven. Satan needed to use more illegal demons to do that. Satan knew if he asked for permission then Carol would see the request for attacking the Crossfire Team and Mark would have been given a warning and would not have gone to Jerusalem."

"Once he had Mark in the room he thought he could ignore God and do as he wished. Once I was informed of the situation I told the Most High of this new transgression by Satan. God called Satan to accounts and Satan had to go before God and try to explain this new breach of covenant. While he was gone, Sarah removed the door to the room and brought Mark out of it. Then we conspired to destroy the room. All of this was done during Satan's absence. He would have come against the three of us with all his power to maintain his control of Mark."

"As things turned out, He was admonished by God for his latest illegal efforts and released. Upon return he found the room destroyed and the resident demons in the pit. The Most High used Satan's techniques on him while he was before Him. He blocked Satan's ability to know what was going on in his kingdom while he was gone. When he returned I hear his anger was monumental. It got even worse when he found out that Mark had legally escaped from his clutches. The devil is very mad about this. He has demanded Mark's return and the replacement of his special room. God has denied him both because of his illegal tactics involving the room."

Raquel smiled broadly. "I have to admit that whenever he attacks the Crossfire Team he loses and not just a few demons, but status. The whole supernatural realm knows that Satan has been foiled again while attacking your team and that is more maddening than anything else to the Lord of the Air. I have now been assigned to your team full time for the foreseeable future. My other duties have been reassigned to others during this time."

Mark smiled, "Welcome aboard, mate. I'm sure the next few things we are going to do will probably require your special skills."

Raquel shook his head. "No doubt, you are going to see if you can make Satan overheat from anger until he explodes, right?"

Mark looked at Jack with a grin and put his hands out palm up to indicate that it was Jack's turn to explain.

Jack nodded his head in agreement. "It appears that after asking God about how to implement the vision he gave me; we have another mission to attack one of Satan's domains. You're definitely invited."

Raquel actually laughed. He stared at the four humans for a few seconds. "I see why the Most High selected you and the members of your team in the first place. He already knew your spirits and that you would definitely prosecute the attack on Satan's domain. Not only because of Satan's use of illegal demons in the human dimension, but because you are willing to do these type of things. I may not survive my association with you but, I believe it will be my finest accomplishment to have been a part of your team."

Raquel continued to smile, "Gabriel has always contended that I am somewhat mentally imbalanced.

Maybe he is right, I believe I'm actually looking forward to this."

Jack sat back and asked, "The first thing we have to determine is how God's Esteem or Righteousness can, flood into the demonic realm and replace the evil that is there now?"

Mark spoke up, "Remember, this isn't going to happen quickly. Raquel, you yourself said it would take years in our time to accomplish the replacement of evil in that domain with God's good."

Sarah said, "Well, like Charlie Wu once said, the longest journey begins with the first step. We need to understand and implement a long term process that will continually advance God's Esteem in that domain and let it do the work over time."

Mark quipped, "Charlie wasn't the first to use that statement. It is actually an ancient Chinese proverb. But, you are right about the first step. Whatever we do has to find fuel in that domain that will allow the fire to grow. Do you have any ideas how we could accomplish that, Raquel?"

Raquel was deep in thought, he nodded his head, "Possibly, I need to talk to Hugo about this."

Laura suggested, "Why don't we pray to the Most High to allow Hugo to speak to all of us about this?"

Raquel said, "I can handle that." He looked into the distance for a brief period. Hugo appeared at the end of the table. Jack noticed that six people were about the maximum for the small conference room. If they were going to add anybody else, they would have to move to a different room.

Hugo grinned at Raquel, "Well, what adventure have you agreed to this time, Raquel?"

Mark explained Jack's dream/vision and their need for advice concerning a self-continuing expansion of God's goodness in the demonic realm.

Hugo blinked several times and didn't say anything for several minutes. Then he brightened up, "I think there could be a way but it will require God's approval and His involvement."

Jack looked at Hugo, "Agreed. We work for Him and this was His vision, so I believe he would want to encourage us to succeed. What are you considering?"

Hugo leaned back in his chair and spread his arms out. "Most High Yahveh, I ask for complete shielding of everything we have talked about and everything we will talk about or do, so that the enemy has no concept of our plans or operations. In Your Honor, Yahveh."

Hugo then leaned forward in a conspiratorial manner. "This is what I think could work and meet your criteria. It will work like one of your computers. We will introduce a virus of goodness into the demonic domain and let it spread."

Mark frowned. "What type of virus?"

Hugo nodded as he said, "I think we should start with several demons and re-institute their original Heavenly alignment through knowledge of their sin and regret of the loss of their higher position."

Laura stared at Hugo. "But, I thought they have been reduced to the demon mentality and shape eons ago by their association with the ultimate evil, Satan. Would they now rebel against him?"

Hugo nodded, "I believe that they would. Some of the angels that were thrown out of Heaven were less than rebellious and got caught up in the action. If we can bring back their memories of the time they were real angels, they could be the catalyst of our virus."

Mark sat up. "Okay Hugo. Three things I don't understand. First, how do we find these marginal demons? Secondly, how do we approach them without battling with them? And most importantly, how do we get them to remember their goodness because they are promised by God that their future is the lake of fire?"

Hugo nodded, "All good questions but not unanswerable."

Laura said, "Aren't we forgetting something? How about Satan and his control of the demons? Don't they have a hierarchy with demons over them who would notice the change in their attitude?"

Hugo nodded again. "We will have to figure a way to inject the virus so that Satan doesn't learn about it and pray that the "good" demons aren't uncovered until they are the majority in their realm. Even then Satan has great power and he might just kill most of his demons to kill the virus. Life in our world and theirs doesn't come with a guarantee.

Jack nodded his head. "We've got to pray and ask God how to create this "virus" and how to administrate it without Satan finding out. We can't ever nurture it because we're not involved in their lives, thank God."

Being angels, Hugo and Raquel immediately sought the Most High for wisdom and guidance. Jack just made himself available if God wanted to speak to him about all of this.

CHAPTER FORTY-FIVE

Hugo sat up and said, "We are done and we have a plan and a virus."

The four humans looked at him expectantly. Mark smiled, "More words Hugo, we need more words about what we have."

Hugo thought for a few seconds. "I have the combination to any of the demon's minds and I have a refreshing for them from the Most High. We simply need to find a demon we don't kill and one of us can pray for the information to be implanted into the demon's mind and it will be done. At the rate demons are being killed, either by us or Satan, we will probably want to do this to as many demons as we can to insure that the virus is planted and will take root. Once the demon knows this truth they can choose another demon to pass it to."

Mark said, "So you have a mentally downloadable virus for any demon that prayer will activate. Is that right?"

Hugo smiled, "Yes, which is allegorically correct."

Jack looked at Hugo, "So, how do we humans do it?"

"You simply pray for the Most High to make the transfer and it will happen. You already have the data in your minds; you got it when I did. God will do the transfer and it is done."

Sarah asked, "How do we pick the demon to transfer it to?" I mean, every stinking one I've met was trying to kill me or run from me so I couldn't kill it. How do we know which ones to imprint?"

Hugo said, "The Most High has a word for you to say to the demon. If it is an acceptable target for the virus it will stop trying to kill you for several seconds. Do the download within those several seconds and let that demon live. The demons that are hopelessly in Satan's grasp will not stop when you say the word. Those you kill."

Laura asked what the word was. Hugo pronounced it several times until everyone there could say the word properly.

Mark frowned, "Hugo, we have to be praying to keep our armor and sword during combat. How do we focus on saying the word and not lose our armor?"

Raquel answered for the teacher. "Just incorporate the word into your battle prayer and when a demon responds, pray for the download as part of your battle prayer. It works, I can assure you."

Jack thought for a bit. "Hugo, could the square pipe I saw in the vision simply be the application of the word and download? I had the impression after Raquel told me about the symbols of the vision that we would have to breach Satan's domain for a second time. I'm confused."

Hugo smiled at Jack. "Jack, the application of symbols from dreams and visions can mean several different things. I am fairly certain that what we have is sufficient to do what your vision shows but there is the possibility that your team may have to brave the demonic realm for a second time, along with using this technique, to start a goodness revolution within Satan's camp."

"I am afraid that Satan is going to try to kidnap one of your people and dare you to save them. If that happens then pray very hard that the Most High will give you the right guidance because the enemy is vile and violent. He will have probably killed the person he kidnapped just so there is no way for you to save them. It would be simply a trap to get you back into his hands."

Mark shook his head. "You know; it is sad that he is protected by prophesy but can do anything he wants to us."

Hugo looked sad, "I know and it isn't fair but that is the way that it is and you have to deal with it. You can't even avoid him because God will counter his illegal moves with your team. I have to go now. Good hunting and may the Most High bless you all and keep you." Hugo disappeared.

Raquel said, "I am going to talk to Carol and find out what she sees in the Matrix. I will return soon. He faded out.

Jack stacked the papers he had in his hands and straightened them out. "Well, it's just us more or less normal humans again. I don't know about you guys but I am going to practice reciting my battle prayer with the two new additions in it. One never knows how soon I'll be in battle again."

Jack really had the new battle prayer down solid because the next call to battle wasn't for three days.

Jack ran into the War Room and asked Laura, "What's the drill?" She said, "We have a supposed group of demons moving to attack a Mossad office downtown. They are barricading the office and getting everyone out that they can. It will take us about nine minutes to get there directly. The Mossad and Kidon flying squads have already left."

Jack stopped and prayed for guidance. His eyes flew open and he told Laura, "Get Su Li or Mike White to fire up an Osprey for lift-off in six minutes. Get your gear and let me talk to Mark right away. Jack was headed toward the Armory when Mark called him. Jack immediately said, "Mark, stand down, you're not going this time and I would prefer that Sarah not go either. I prayed and this is a trap to get you and Sarah. Stay with Ethan so that you can advise me, Charlie, or David but, please, stay here this time. Pray about it and you'll understand. Malone out."

Jack and Laura ran up the rear ramp which was being raised at the same time. Jack moved up and squatted down in front of David, Charlie and Linda Wu. "Listen, I ordered Mark and probably Sarah not to be a part of this melee. I prayed and the Father told me that this was a multipronged attack with the goals of finding and killing Elon, plus looking to capture Mark and Sarah with the emphasis on Mark. Keep your wits sharp and avoid getting grabbed and beaten to death, okay? Stay in groups of three or four if you can. Pass the word to the other troops. We're only supposed to have a dozen demons but I would count on three times that many. Have you all practiced putting the code word in you battle prayer? Good, I will see you after we dispatch this horde."

He thought it over and told David, "Take Alexis and Megan and find and defend Elon. I think I know why he's on their hit list."

The Osprey was dropping towards the streets of downtown when they started taking ground fire. The armor was keeping the bullets outside but Su Li didn't like the incoming fire one bit. She stopped dropping and swung the right side toward the people firing at them. The two .50

Caliber heavy machine guns cut loose and devastated the humans with the demons.

Su Li then set the Tilt Rotor down in the street and shut it down. She jumped out of the pilot's seat and ran for the ramp. She started praying as she went down the ramp and her armor and sword flashed into golden fire. She spotted Jack and Laura already in the battle and headed for them. She thought to herself, "I need to mention this adrenaline overload from Holy Anger when I'm trying to fly the freaking plane." She cut down three demons without breaking stride. She attacked several of the demons battling with Jack and Laura.

Jack saw her and yelled, "Su Li, what are you doing here?"

Su Li yelled back, "You said groups of three or four. You and Laura make only two so I'm your third." She started vocally reciting her battle prayer and concentrating on killing demons. Despite the number she fought the Holy Anger kept growing as she worked harder to increase the rate of dead demons. She started to use her martial arts skills and it made it easier to kill a demon and move on to the next one. She saw one demon that stopped when she said the code word and because she had made it a trained reflex she prayed that the Father would transfer the virus download to that demon. She side kicked the demon and it fell down and got lost in the fighting.

Jack was also feeling the power increasing along with the level of the Holy Anger and he went into Time Compression, High Speed and reduced the number of blows he was delivering but making each one count. Laura was right beside him as he cleared a large space of demons. He saw that the field was quickly emptying of the demonic forces. He went to high guard with Su Li and Laura back to back with him. But there were no more demons to fight. The rift had closed and several of the other warriors were cleaning up any remaining demons.

Jack stopped praying and his armor and sword disappeared when one of the supposedly dead demons lifted its head and said. "uwaatt woordidd youusay" in a deep and guttural voice. Jack was about to pray for his armor when Laura put her hand on his and said the code word in a loud voice. The demon swung its ugly head toward Laura and said "yesssss". Laura prayed that the Father would apply the virus to the demon.

The demon stopped moving and Jack watched to see that it didn't reach for the black sword near its right hand. He saw the demon's head nod twice and it turned its vision on Jack and then faded away.

Jack blew out a big breath. "Wow! That was something different." Standing straight up Jack called David on the battle COMM.

David came back right away. "Jack, we were able to keep the demons away from Elon. He is all right. Is it all right to come out?"

Jack confirmed the end of the battle. He took a quick count from everybody and called Carol. "Carol, did you see any approval by God for eighty-nine demons to attack in Tel Aviv?"

Carol replied, "No, Jack. There were only eleven requests for demons in the human dimension and those were not going to Tel Aviv."

Jack thanked her. He walked several feet away and yelled into the air. "RAQUEL". Raquel appeared next to Jack. "Yes, Jack, I know. I've already reported to the Most High about the illegal demons you and your team were fighting today."

Jack shook his head. "Raquel, I know you're doing your best to assist us but we have to get a handle on this conflict stuff before we are overwhelmed and destroyed. I really thought the Father was going to come down on Satan for continuing to ignore God's orders to stop bringing illegal demons into the human world."

Raquel looked at Jack for a few seconds. "Were you not interested in spreading the virus? This is the only venue where your people and demons can meet and not be suspected by Satan."

Jack sighed. "That is true but I don't want to lose my team members in large numbers just to do that. Please temper the number of demons Satan can throw at us at one time. Please."

Raquel nodded his head. "I would speak to the Most High but, I believe he wants to talk to you now."

Jack was about to get on his knees when he was suddenly in Heaven. He stood there in demon stain and sweat and waited.

Light flooded the place where Jack stood. There was great power in the light and it refreshed him completely. He stood taller and closed his eyes. Expecting to perhaps meet Yahshua again, Jack was amazed when Yahveh spoke to him.

"My child, rest and listen to Me. I am Yahveh, your God and I am proud of you and your team for your willingness to do battle in My name and for My Kingdom. I understand your frustration and concerns. Because of Satan's continual flagrant violations of my commandments, I have now limited Satan so that he can no more move his illegal demons into the human dimension. He believes in his pride that he can continue to disregard Me but I created him and the fallen angels. He now must get My approval to allow even one of his demons to pass into the world of men. Satan knows that Carol can see all of his plans to use his demons against the Crossfire Team and so he will use his Earthly tools in attempts to stop your team and or kill all of you, especially Carol. There will be many assassins recruited to do just that. Satan will use his tool, Marco Marino and the RHONE troops, to hunt your team. He will make the RHONE use their assassins and those he can buy from the world over. But! They will not be victorious. I will fight for your team with a love and power that surpasses any care and concern ever known in the world of man."

"I have many plans for you, your wife, and the other team members because to meet prophesy and all righteousness there are things I need men and women to do and also to pray for Heaven's intervention. Know that I have sharpened and honed your team to the sharpest edge of human capability so that you can do what I need to be done. You see a very small segment of human history and I see time's beginning and every detail until it ends. Stand strong and rally your troops to battle and you will be victorious in My Name. See, I have told you so that when it comes to pass you will know that I am God."

Jack watched as the sun faded out and he found himself standing alone on the recent battlefield. It had gotten dark and he knew his wife would be concerned. He used his battle comm to call Laura.

She answered with a worried voice. "Jack! Where are you?" Ethan couldn't find your medallion until just a second ago. I've got transport headed your way. What happened?"

Jack spoke strongly but calmly. "I'm fine Laura; Yahveh wanted a one-on-one with me in Heaven. That's why you couldn't locate me. I'm sorry but, it happened before I could tell you."

She said, "Oh thank God. I was worried Old Nick might have grabbed you thinking you were Mark. Listen; be wary until you get your ride."

Jack looked around, "Not to worry, dear. I seem to have a protecting angel hovering over me. I'll see you soon. Malone out."

Jack looked to his left. "Are you doing all right Elon?"

Elon walked out of the shadows where he was standing watching the area around Jack. He walked up to Jack and smiled, "What sharp little eyes you have."

Jack laughed. "Not really that sharp. I saw the reflection of the street light on your weapon and asked God if I should be worried. He said "No". The rest of it was simple deduction as to who would be standing in the bushes outside of a Mossad office. Thank you for protecting me."

CHAPTER FORTY-SIX

The Apache helicopter settled down with Su Li's signature landing. She would come in at one hundred miles per hour and bring it to a dead stop, in the last fifty feet, right at the ground.

Jack cleared his M8 combat rifle and got in the passenger seat. "Hello Su Li. Thanks for coming to get me."

Su Li smiled at him although it was hard to see with the combat helmet, NVG and the automated firing control in front of her face. She pulled pitch and revved the engine so that they went straight up until she cleared all the houses and wires. She tipped the chopper over to the left and checked with Ethan on clearance. He came back with a thirty-three-minute hold for satellite observation. Jack said, "Just put it on the top Mossad landing pad and we'll have them move it down when it is clear."

Su Li nodded her head and then said, "Jack I have a bit of a problem that you might solve for me." She looked at Jack and he smiled at her. "We need to do something about the adrenaline overload from Holy Anger when I'm trying to fly a freaking plane! Anyway, that was the way I was thinking before the battle today."

Jack frowned, "I see, that is why you were working out your anger in demon piñatas on the battleground today. I see your point. It would be hard for me to drive a car with that much Holy Anger pumping up my system. I'll rotate you and Mike with one of you going to fight riding in the back. If things get too hectic then I will get a Mossad pilot and both of you can ride in the back."

Su Li talked to the MA'AM (Mossad Aviation Assets Manager) and brought the helicopter into a perfect landing on the elevated pad behind the Portal.

After transiting the base, Jack walked into the Armory and went through the routine. He filled out his After Action report and sent it to Ethan. He realized that things had gotten heavy right in the middle of switching from Charlie/Linda to Ethan/Crayton. "I'd better check on how Ethan is holding up."

Walking into the COMSEC area he spotted Ethan sitting in Charlie's old office at the computer. Checking his watch, he saw it was almost ten o'clock in the evening. He walked over and tapped on the door to the office. Ethan looked over and punched the button on his console that unlocked the door.

Jack walked over to the desk and asked Ethan how he was holding up. Ethan turned away from the computer keyboard and thought for a few seconds. "Actually, quite well considering the "Assistant/Counselor" I have. Charlie created a really great alter-ego in Crayton and then customized it to be everything for me. I was surprised this morning when I finally fooled Crayton. I had to go to the bathroom and he didn't pick up on that. Actually, that's rather trivial. We make a good team, I come up with the ideas, and he sees if I have the time in my schedule and then does all the heavy lifting. Do you know I could have shaved more than half my time off finding Su Li if I'd had Crayton then?"

Jack said, "Well you look good but what are you doing here after 10 at night?"

Ethan smiled, "Personal project I have been thinking about for a while. I'll give you a hint. Inspector Clueso is officially back at work for us and he is triple armor plated from being detected plus he has complete access to anything without tripping any internal alarms when he checks files, thanks to Crayton."

Jack nodded, "I see this job suits you. Okay, Ethan, make sure you attend the Core Team meetings and if available I want you kicking demon butt in the field with the rest of us. You've had eyes on Napoleon and can tag him easily. Although, there is an additional requirement. You have to talk to him before you kill him."

Ethan's eyebrows went up at that. "Oh, Really?"

Jack said, "I'll fill you in at the next Core Team meeting."

Ethan asked, "How come Charlie could be the fly on the wall and I have to be there in person?"

Jack said, "Because I have to pray for you and it's hard to put my hand on your doppelganger."

Ethan thought about that, smiled and said, "That is very true, I'll be there."

Jack went back to his apartment and found Laura doing her evening exercises while she waited for him. "Hi Sweetie, how are you doing after your combat exercises today?"

She grinned and stopped exercising. "I'm fine and I'm glad I got to download the goodness message to a demon. Do you think he'll make it home?"

Jack slowly shook his head. "I have no concept what life in that domain is like. I hope he sees the opportunity this offers him and others like him."

She frowned and said "I can only hope that he makes it and gets a chance to spread the message."

CHAPTER FORTY-SEVEN

Mark found Jack the next morning hard at work on a Martial Arts Wooden Dummy. Mark watched Jack as he tirelessly struck and kicked the dummy in many different combinations of hand, arm, and foot attacks.

After Jack finished, Mark approached him and asked if they could talk. Jack nodded and got a towel to wipe the sweat off of his head, neck and arms. Jack sat down next to Mark and raised an eyebrow in a silent question.

Mark smiled, "I was really surprised yesterday when you told me to stand down. I think that was the first time I had ever been told not to fight. I've thought about it quite a bit since then and I prayed about it. I understand your reasoning especially after Raquel talked to me this morning.

"I believe the enemy is trying to make me take offense at your shutting me down even if it was for my own good. That was until around 3A.M. this morning when Yahveh God woke me up and told me to pray for my life. I did as he asked and while I was in prayer God showed me the trap that Satan had arranged for me. Jack, I would have been taken again if I had been there! Not only would they have captured me but they would have gotten Sarah, too. Now I have a quandary; I trust the Lord and God and don't want to be disobedient but I feel that I need to be by your side facing the enemy. Then I realized what you felt like when I went to Hell without you or Laura and it just about broke my heart. I came here this morning to tell you that I am sorry if my going without you caused you pain."

Jack reached over and put his arm around Mark's shoulders. "I know exactly how you feel. I feel that way, too. But, and I repeat, "But", I have no feelings about being abandoned or anything. I know we probably can't do what we do without you and Sarah. Yesterday morning, I knew beyond a shadow of a doubt that if you went, you would be taken and eventually killed. You of all people know that I can't see the future but God can and he showed me you and Sarah being taken. Then I tried my best to intervene and free you only to have both myself and Laura killed as they took you and Sarah away."

Jack felt tears in his eyes. "You see; I was willing to give my life to rescue you but it wouldn't have helped. Both Laura and I died and Satan still had you and Sarah. That's when I told you to stand down. I know it makes me seem weak but I can't keep doing this without you by my side. I'm not strong enough by myself. Together we can topple mountains. Still, if God warns me about your capture or death I will make the same choices. I want you to always be a part of this team."

Mark looked at Jack and saw the tears and he couldn't help but cloud up himself. "Thanks for being strong when you had to, buddy. I will never forget it. As far as I know you and I will walk into Heaven together with our wives. Ooh Rah!"

Jack tipped his head, "Isn't that a Marine Corp saying?"

Mark grinned lopsidedly, "So what? If they want to complain about my use of it, they need to meet a couple demons and see what we do. I can guarantee that they will make us honorary Marines for life. Ooh Rah!"

Jack grinned, "Ooh Rah!"

Jack sat back and looked into the future. He looked at Mark, "You want to reprise your role in the Road to Hell mission?"

Mark laughed, "In two words, Hell No! I have made a very serious personal enemy out of Satan and if he found me in his backyard again I dread to think of the heights he would go to just to beat me to death personally. Why do you ask?"

Jack told Mark about his visit to Heaven and his learning what was happening from God Himself. He thought for a few minutes. "Mark, you know we have seriously changed Elon's life and made him a target for those demons yesterday. I'm afraid that he is somewhat lost between two worlds and we need to see what we can do to help him."

Mark thought about that and said, "We first need to pray and see what the Father wants us to do. Then we need to ask my wife what she thinks. Being Jewish to begin with and having made the jump to Messianic Jew gives her a unique viewpoint which could relate better than our Judeo-Christian backgrounds."

Jack said, "Good call, buddy. Let us pray and see what God says first." The two warriors bent their heads and called out to God for guidance and wisdom.

CHAPTER FORTY-EIGHT

Jack and Laura sat with Mark and Sarah as they all finished lunch in the food court near the War Room. After the guys cleared the dishes and wiped the table down they sat down and looked at Sarah.

Aware of their attention Sarah looked at them with a crooked grin on her face. "What?"

Mark asked her what she thought of the position that Elon was in with his history and the sudden introduction to Yahshua and a whole new paradigm.

Sarah thought about it for a few seconds. She sat forward in her chair. "As I see it, right now, Elon is trapped in a do-and-die situation. His whole history has been Kidon. Now he has to choose between what he knows is the truth or his life before Yahshua. He's sure he'll lose his job once he announces his decision to follow the Son of God. He probably doesn't have a fallback position and he can't sell his talents anywhere because either the Kidon will kill him or his new bosses will attempt to drain him of all his Kidon knowledge which he is sworn to never reveal. It is a terrible choice and isn't getting any better as time goes by. What do you think we could do to help him?"

Jack looked at Sarah. "Mark and I spent some time with the Father about that very question. I believe our leading is that we are bound to help him since we essentially got him into the situation. My question is, where is his loyalty if we hire him?"

Sarah ruefully smiled, "That's a really good question. I know that all his training and time in service was based on total loyalty to Israel and to the Mossad, but above that is loyalty to the Kidon. Would we be just moving his problem from one crisis to another by offering to bring him into the Crossfire Team?"

Jack had been silently praying about that and got a definite leading. "I don't think so. As long as we don't try to get anything about the Kidon or Mossad from him I believe he could be as loyal to us as he has been to them. I personally think he would prefer to die than break any loyalty he gives to anyone. As long as we don't become enemies or competitors with the Mossad or the Kidon I don't think there will be a problem. We might have a problem if our goal is to watch somebody that the Kidon has ordered killed. Will he follow our orders or revert to the Kidon's orders?"

Laura stood up. "Let's try it and see if we can live with him. Supposing, of course, he decides to join us at all."

Jack used his cell phone and called Elon and asked him to come over to the Crossfire Team side of the base. Laura said that she would go out and bring him back to the table.

The other three members discussed what Elon's role would be in the Team. Laura walked up with Elon who shook hands all around. Sarah was comforted by the fact that he didn't check the number of fingers he still had after shaking hands with her.

Jack went and got soft drinks or coffee for each of them. After some social chit-chat Jack asked Elon how things were going.

Elon looked at each of the people at the table and realized he couldn't snow them. "It has been very trying the last few days. I'm trying to get up the courage to tell my team that I have given my life to Yahshua. I sincerely doubt that they will believe me. Then when they know it's true they will shun me and have nothing to do with me. It seems such a terrible abandonment to both them and I. I know I have to do it, I'm just not sure how."

Sarah nodded, "I know Elon, I went through that exact thing when Yahshua brought David Zahavy back to life in Tel Aviv. I think I can safely say that I made the right decision.

Elon laughed a hollow laugh. "That's not my problem. I already made my decision about that. And I am going to tell my friends and leaders about that decision. I'm now afraid that they will never listen to me about the reality of Christ and they will end up in Hell. That, plus, I will be unemployed and probably marked for death because of what I know about the Kidon. It is definitely a mess."

Jack caught Elon's eye. "What if we hired you? Would your team and leaders accept your promise of loyal silence? Could you be loyal to our organization and still work with them on joint ventures? I do know we pay better than they do and you would be even busier than in the Kidon." Jack looked at Sarah."Also, we hired a Mossad Assassin before and it worked out for everybody."

Elon looked at Sarah and thought through all the possibilities. He smiled, "It just might work for lots of reasons, but, primarily because if I leave to join you they will believe I am moving up." He looked at the other people at the table. "There I go giving away Kidon secrets all ready. Yes, they all think very highly of your team and the war you fight." He looked at Jack. "What position would I fill?"

Jack said, "With your experience I see three positions you could assist us in right now. The first would be as a warrior. I've seen your valor and guts and I know that you would be a great warrior for God. The second would be as a team leader and one of our Core Team working with the SOG troops. They need the real world experience you have and they already like you. The third position would be as another liaison between our team and the Mossad. You would also give us better coordination with the Kidon when and when we go to war together against the enemy again."

Elon thought that over. If his team mates approve of his move to the Crossfire Team, that would make it much easier in the future, because those guys and gals were destined to become the leadership in the Kidon in the next few years, if they lived. He sighed, "There are some really bright people in the Kidon, I'm fairly sure that they'll figure out my change in religion right away."

Sarah nodded, "I agree, but it might make them even more upset what God has told me and it was confirmed by Rabbi Ben Channon that all Jews are going to be shown the truth about Yahshua soon. If you'll promise not to tell anyone but us, I'll tell you a secret."

Elon nodded his head, "I swear I'll not tell anyone. You've got my word on that."

Sarah was serious, "Rabbi Ben Channon has met Yahshua and admits He is the Messiah. He knows it will not matter in a short while as G-d will prove to all Jews that Yahshua is His Son and the first born as well as their Savior."

Elon realized that it didn't shock him that the leading teacher of Judaism was a follower of Yahshua. "How will the Jews ever give up their religion and their beliefs?"

Sarah smiled, "They don't have to. Once they know the truth about Yahshua and the deception becomes meaningless, they will continue with everything the Torah says but embrace Yahshua. In a few years they'll swear that they always knew it was true.

Elon smiled, "Okay, I will accept employment with your group; if you can match my salary requirements of my present job."

Sarah choked on her soft drink, coughed a few times and then broke out in laughter. She looked at Elon, "You make about 525,000 Israeli New Shekels per year with bonuses, right?"

Elon said, "Roughly that much, maybe a little more, a little less."

Jack smiled at Elon. "As a member of the Core Team you will make a base salary of Israeli 3.5 million New Shekels per year with bonuses that will probably triple that amount. But, if you demand we match your present salary I can arrange that."

Elon held up his hand for a few seconds. "Please, give me a chance to get my heart started again. Well, since you put it that way I'll remove the demand to match my present salary."

Everyone laughed at that. Elon looked up at Jack and Mark with obvious gratitude. "I accept your offer of employment and thank you very much. Jack handed Elon his computer tablet. All the information was already filled in. All he had to do was sign it which he did.

After another round of handshakes Elon said, "Well, I had better go tell my team and my boss about this."

Mark said, "Tell your team about the salary and they will be forever envious. Let me tell your bosses about this. I will start with the Prime Minister and work my way down through the Mossad and finally the Kidon. I'll tell them that we wanted a man with your skills and dedication and that we'll make sure your info confidentiality is confirmed and not breached. In fact, anything you don't want to reveal we don't want to know about. Okay?"

Sarah grinned, "For right now, don't bring up your decision to follow Yahshua. Eventually, after the truth is shown about Yahshua, it will become a non-issue and until then you're just working with us and it will turn out to be a good thing for the Kidon as well as us.

CHAPTER FORTY-NINE

Jack called a complete Core Team Meeting which included Ethan and Elon. Jack introduced Elon to the Core Team and announced his position and authorities as a team leader.

Mark then let the Core Team know about the latest information that Jack had heard from Yahveh and stressed the fact that Satan is pushing the RHONE SS troops to assassinate anyone involved with the Crossfire Team and they were apparently hiring every gun for hire in the Middle East as a secondary force to assassinate the team.

Elon said, "Aahh, you didn't mention that little point." There was a great deal of laughter at that point.

Jack told the Core Team he wanted them to stress the danger to the SOG warriors and attempt to keep them out of the RHONE SS's gun sights.

Jack told them if they had to go out they had to wear full body armor and in groups of no less than three.

After the meeting, Jack introduced Elon to the SOG team that he was going to command. Jack assured the SOG troops that Yahveh had appointed Elon to help train them and direct their activities in the field and on the battlefield.

Elon was elated with his new position and confided in Mark that the Kidon had far less to work with in the way of technology than the Crossfire Team. David agreed with that sentiment.

Mark called Jack and Laura, Sarah, David and Alexis, Charlie and Linda, Ethan, and Elon to a second meeting.

Mark started the conversation. "I want to figure out how we are going to find, identify, and kill all of the RHONE SS troops assigned to kill us. I, for one, do not want to sit down here in fear that someone will use a sniper rifle and punch my lights out as soon as I go above ground. We need to get a grip on how many assassins we are faced with and get photos of them and send out two or three counter-assassin groups. If we eliminate enough of them, I believe that they will run."

Jack asked Charlie and Ethan to see if they could penetrate RHONE'S computer systems and get the necessary information about their secretive attackers. He also asked them to see if they could find out who the contract assassins were.

Jack sent a message to the IDF, the Mossad, and to the Kidon with the information about the assassins.

Jack immediately identified three ten member groups that would work in eight hour shifts to draw out and eliminate the assassins.

Raquel showed up and Jack explained what they were doing. Raquel nodded his head and made a few suggestions which were adopted by the counter assassin groups.

Elon walked in and Jack introduced him to Raquel. They shook hands and Elon walked over to Mark and said, "Raquel is a big guy. I wouldn't want to be on opposite sides in a battle. Mark looked up and said, "You definitely don't want to cross swords with him. He is an Archangel."

Elon turned and looked at Raquel again. "Really? He is really an Archangel?" Mark nodded his head.

Charlie came back into the War Room and handed a package of photos to Jack. "I've got to hand it to Ethan; he slipped into the RHONE computer complex in Bern, and was able to get the photos of all of their SS troops. We're already doing facial recognition on the borders of Israel and will let you know when and where we find them."

Mark said, "Let's work on the ones closest to us and then work outward in a concentric circle to find all of them. At least we should concentrate on the ones in Israel to begin with."

Mark made up a list of the ten people that would step out into the public arena starting at 10 P.M. tonight. He worked on the other two lists for the 5:00 A.M. to 1:00P.M. shift and the 1:00 P.M. to 9:00 P.M. shift tomorrow night. He stood up. "Remember; set your area after we locate one or more of these turkeys. Six Counter-snipers to your nests first, then the two support and backup personnel and last the two targets. Snipers will be Mark, Carol, Sarah, and I, Ethan, Charlie, and Linda Wu. Support personnel will be Megan and Laura. The targets will be David and Alexis. Targets, try to act like you are being cautious but if the assassination attempt is up-close and personal, just kill them. Also, remember that they are also hiring contract assassins and we don't have any photos of them."

CHAPTER FIFTY

Ethan called Mark on the Combat COMM System. "Mark, I have three positive facial recognition responses. All three are within six blocks of the Portal on Trumpeldor St. Apparently they suspect we work out of here despite our efforts to hide that fact. This looks to be a coordinated effort between the assassins. Use your Combat Reticule and I'll place the photos of those three there. I will try to track them but there aren't that many cameras available."

Mark said, "Link those photos and grab your sniper rifle and let's get to our nests." Mark indicated which sniper was to be on which building and at what level. "Make sure you've got a green light from either Jack or me before firing."

The six counter-snipers left at separate times and quickly acquired their "nests" for sniping. Then Megan and Laura left with their support vehicles that the Mossad had ready for them. Once they were in place the signal came for the targets to move.

David grinned and looked at his wife, Alexis, "Show time for us, dear." They exited the Portal through a side entrance and approached the target zone from a different direction.

Alexis spoke quietly on the Combat microphone. "We are just coming onto the north end of the target zone on Trumpeldor Street on the east side of the street. We have nothing to report as yet."

Since night had fallen, the six counter-snipers were using magnified NVG'S to search for the assassins. Two took the buildings on the west side of Trumpeldor Street. Two more took the east side and the last two scanned the street around the targets.

All the counter-snipers were outfitted with M81 A1A Barrett .50 Caliber sniper rifles. These rifles can be fired accurately at one mile and one and a half miles. Some kill shots have been made at over two miles with these rifles. The fact that these rifles were designed to destroy vehicles at that range made them more than lethal to human troops.

As David and Alexis had walked to their third block Ethan said over the COMM NET. "I have a target." He zeroed in the rifle. "Assassin #21 is on the building across from me two floors below my nest. He is in a window with a rifle pointed at the targets. I have a solution, awaiting a green light."

Mark told him, "I confirm his ID. You have a green light. Take him out."

Ethan fired the silenced rifle and the round took the shooter in the forehead, slapping him back into the room. He dropped the rifle as he was hit and the rifle fell but landed on a roof on the first floor. Mark gave the location to the Mossad Communications Center so that they could collect it.

David spoke up. "I have Assassin #62 on the ground roughly eighty feet in front of us against the wall under the awing that says "Chappell's" in English."

Carol said, "I've got her. I have a solution, awaiting a green light."

Mark said, "If she makes a threatening move, you have a green light. Shoot to kill."

As David and Alexis came within thirty feet of the woman assassin, she stepped out and started to bring out an Uzi machine pistol.

Carol's rifle coughed and the round slammed the woman up against the wall with a large blood splatter. She fell to the sidewalk and didn't move.

Alexis felt the unction of the Holy Spirit and she ducked. A bullet slammed into a car right behind her. Ethan's snap shot answered the assassin with a shot through the gut which caused the man to collapse forward out of the window and the body fell all the way to the sidewalk six floors below. While the body didn't strike any of the people; it did cause a small panic in the area.

Mark was on the rooftop of a building a block away from the action when he came under fire that was too close for comfort. He looked up and saw two men walking toward him firing rifles.

Mark rolled to his left into the shelter of an air conditioner housing. He aimed his rifle and shot first one and then the other man with his M81 A1A sniper rifle. The rounds cored their chests and threw them backward in lifeless heaps on the roof top. Mark called out. "Be aware there are assassin backups in and on the buildings. If you are attacked, locate and destroy the backups."

Mark went over to the two dead assassins and confirmed their identities. They were both armed as the assassins but weren't on the list that he could remember. He took photos with his phone. As he turned back a large demon appeared and tried to smash Mark with a monstrous club. Mark moved backward quickly and the club missed. Mark shot the creature two times without effect. He started to pray his combat prayer and his armor and sword flashed into existence. He attacked the demon and cut off the arm with the club. While he battled the creature he added to his previous announcement, "Demons are defending the assassins, also." It wasn't much of a match. Mark was able to cut the demon's head off in one swipe as it tried to hit him with its remaining arm.

Some of the other counter-snipers were set upon by other assassins or demons. The advance warning gave the Team members a serious edge. Most of this action went unnoticed by the majority of the Tel Aviv population.

On the street below, Alexis started praying and her golden armor and the Sword of the Word, flowing with the Esteem of Yahveh, exploded into view as she charged a demon that manifested. She danced away from its sword and then slammed her sword blade through the demon's throat and twisted the blade for maximum effect. That demon dissipated into black smoke and disappeared. David was dispatching a demon that had attacked him. Two more demons suddenly appeared behind Alexis and tried to force her against a store wall. That ended quickly when Megan showed up in her gold armor behind the demons. The demons quickly lost the battle with the two women. The warrior's armor and swords disappeared as the demons were all gone.

Mark told David and Alexis to get back to the Portal without being seen if possible. He then called the rest of the team to do the same.

David and Alexis parted company and disappeared into the crowd which was swirling around from concern about the fallen man and the lack of gunshots. The rest of the team assembled at the support trucks and returned without incident.

CHAPTER FIFTY-ONE

After everyone had returned they cleaned up their weapons, and themselves; dictated their after action reports, then they met in the War Room.

After reviewing the combat camera records and the after-action reports, Jack tallied the damage. "We had to fight fourteen demons and seven assassins! On top of that, four of the demons were illegally in the human dimension. I think the other side wanted to draw us out and eliminate us with overload tactics again."

Mark was nodding, "You've got that right. They were ready for us and would have killed us except for God. They trumped our trump and had assassins and demons hunting the hunters. We need a better plan and a better detection capability before we get major injuries and deaths on our side of the dance card."

Jack shook his head, "We can't keep this routine up because we will lose people eventually. There has to be a better way to hunt these assassins. Mark killed two of the contract assassins and we don't know how many more there are of them either."

Laura prayed and asked Yahveh why there were still illegal demons on the Earth. She heard a still, quiet voice tell her that those demons were already on the earth when the ban was instituted.

Laura got everyone's attention. "Guys, these assassins are out-thinking us and we need to get ahead of them quickly. They figured out what we were going to do and they set up a double trap. God says that the demons that were here illegally were already in our dimension before Yahveh shut them down from entering it."

Mark prayed his thanks to a loving God that would allow the team members to survive the multiple assassins and demons. He knew they had to find a way to combat these tactics. He agreed that they would perish by sheer overload. Mark slumped into his chair. "I know that they are reading our mail somehow. I just don't know how."

Jack sighed. I agree, but I don't think any of the Crossfire Team is a traitor. I'll bet we have a demonic spy here somewhere reporting on everything we do. Let's get Raquel here and have him and his angels start hunting demon spies."

The Crossfire Team will return in

"Assassins Crossfire"

If this story has awakened you or moved you to seek the love of Christ and His power for your life, whether you've never accepted Jesus as your savior or you've fallen away, repeat the following prayer and begin a most wonderful journey into eternal life with Him today.

Father God in heaven, As You said in Your Holy Word, (Romans 10:9) that if we confess the Lord our God and believe in our hearts that God raised Jesus from the dead, we shall be saved.

(The prayer on the next page is a sample prayer when asking Jesus into your heart as your Savior. You can also pray this in your own words.)

Salvation Prayer

Dear God in heaven, I come to you in the name of Jesus. I confess to You that I am a sinner, and I am sorry for my sins and the life that I have lived; I need your forgiveness. I believe that your only begotten Son Jesus Christ shed His precious blood on the cross at Calvary and died for my sins, and I am now willing to turn from my sin.

Right now I confess Jesus as the Lord of my life and my soul. With all my heart, I truly believe that your Holy Spirit raised Jesus from the dead. Today I accept Jesus Christ as my personal Savior and according to Your Word, right now I am saved.

I thank you Jesus, for your unlimited grace which has saved me from my sins. I thank you Jesus that your grace that never leads to license, but rather it always leads to repentance. Therefore Lord Jesus, transform my life so that I may bring glory and honor to you alone and not to myself.

I Thank you Lord Jesus, for dying for me at Calvary and giving me eternal life.

Amen.

If you just said this prayer and you meant it with all your heart, believe that you are now saved and have been born again.

You may ask, "Now that I am saved, what do I do next?" First of all you need to get into a spirit-filled, bible-based church that teaches the Scriptures, and you need to study God's Word.

Once you have found a church home, you will want to become water-baptized. By accepting Christ you are baptized in the spirit, but it is through water-baptism that you publically announce your obedience to the Lord Jesus. Water baptism is a symbol of your salvation from the dead. You were dead but now you live, for Jesus Christ has redeemed you for a price! The price was His atoning death on the cross. May God Bless You!

www.ingramcontent.com/pod-product-compliance
Lightning Source LLC
Chambersburg PA
CBHW060936180626
46817CB00004B/1581